Murder

in the

Boonies

A Sleuth Sisters Mystery
BY MAGGIE PILL

Book Layout ©2013 BookDesignTemplates.com

Cover Art by Yocladesigns: http://yocladesigns.com

Gwendolyn Press

Port Huron, MI 48060

Murder in the Boonies/Maggie Pill — 1st ed.

ISBN 978-0-9861475-0-0

CHAPTER ONE

Faye

When my kids were growing up, I taught them to be hard-working, loyal, and kind to small children and animals. I never stopped to think that those things can lead to heartache—and in a few instances can get you killed.

It started with a phone call. Before I could say a word, my sister started talking, her voice ringing with indignation, "Our renters are gone, and they gave me no notice whatsoever!"

"What do you mean, Retta? McAdams moved out?"

"I got a letter in today's mail, saying they were leaving on Monday. They didn't send me notice until the day they left."

"Maybe it got delayed somehow."

"The letter's dated the same day as the postmark." She gave a ladylike snort. (Everything Retta does is ladylike.) "I'll never show it to Barbara Ann. It's so full of errors she'd have apoplexy. Can you imagine just sending a letter to say you're moving away and leaving the same day?" She paused for breath. "I'm shocked, Faye. I never imagined those people would do something like this!"

Retta has the dubious honor of managing our family farm. After our parents died, first Dad, then Mom a year later, none of us wanted to live there. Barb was out in Tacoma, and Retta and Don had just built a nice home on the river. I had to stay in town since my husband Dale needs to be close to medical and rehab services.

I loved the old place, and selling it to strangers didn't seem right, so I'd argued we should rent it out. Retta, who loves to be in charge of things, agreed to manage the property. She leased the fields to a local farmer and the house and outbuildings to a series of tenants. Ten miles out of Allport with a house that isn't exactly a palace, the farm's renters hadn't stayed long until McAdams—I thought his first name was Ben—moved in. McAdams had come to Allport a single man just out of the military, rented the house and outbuildings from Retta, and brought in chickens and a few cattle. Later he'd found a girlfriend, a woman with three little girls, and since then the menagerie had grown to include other interesting creatures like reindeer and peafowl.

"I thought they were happy out there with their critters."

"I did too," Retta replied. "Rose is always really good about sending the rent money on time. But I've been busy planning summer events for the Chamber and VBS at church. With that and helping you two at the agency, I haven't been out there in a while."

Retta is part of the Smart Detective Agency only through sheer will on her part. Our older sister Barb and I started the business with the idea that we would solve crimes and help people. Retta noses her way into our business whenever possible, as she has since we were teenagers and she was the little sister we didn't want along on our adventures.

I have to admit she's often useful. The widow of a state policeman killed in the line of duty, Retta has contacts Barb and I don't. She also has a sharp intellect and plenty of courage. On the down-side, she's impulsive and bossy, which irks Barb all the time and me sometimes. Barb keeps reminding me—and Retta, too—that she's an auxiliary employee, not a partner. That doesn't stop Retta from acting as if she runs the place.

Still upset about our renters' disappearance, Retta went on with her news. "I talked to Chet Masters, the guy who farms our fields. He said not only are they gone, but they left their animals behind."

"What?"

"I know! Half a dozen reindeer, a flock of peacocks, some chickens, and three or four cows. There could be more. I never paid much attention."

"And they didn't make arrangements for them?"

"None. Masters peeked in the windows, and he says there's a lot of stuff still in the house too." Retta's voice rose as her irritation spiked again. "How inconsiderate can people be? I'll have to find someone to clean the place out before I can run ads and get new tenants in."

"Don't rent it if it's too much work." The regular deposits in my bank account were nice, but the agency had started picking up steam. "Since Dale and I moved in with Barb, we can manage without the money."

Retta made a coughing sound, as if I'd suggested she do the Dance of the Seven Veils to spice up the opening of Vacation Bible School. "A house falls apart ten times faster when it's empty, Faye. We need to find renters this summer, fall at the latest. Nobody wants to move in the middle of a Michigan winter."

After a little more grousing about ungrateful people, Retta ended the call, already planning how she would fit re-renting the house into her busy schedule. I might have suggested she give up a tanning session or two and save herself skin damage down the road, but I learned long ago such comments bring little sniffs of disapproval. Ladylike sniffs, since they come from Retta.

Forgetting the call for the moment, I returned to the robbery case Barb and I were working on. Searching online sites, I checked pawn and secondhand shops in hopes of finding goods our client was missing. It was tedious work, but one hit could break a case.

When Barb came in and I told her about our disappearing renters, she showed little interest. We both trusted Retta to see that the property was maintained, the taxes and insurance paid, and our shares of after-expense money deposited in our bank accounts. For Retta, our renters' flight was exasperating. For Barb it was just a curious anecdote. For me, any mention of the farm brought a vague sense of longing for the past.

Barb spent her professional career as an assistant D.A. on the West Coast, and for her, the farm is just a pleasant childhood memory. Retta stayed in Allport, but from somewhere around the age of ten, she resented living in the country. She complained about being so far from her friends and the bright lights of the city, if Allport's modest size and average number of street lights can be considered that way. Neither of my sisters has the emotional attachment to the farm I have.

For me, the farm is home, the place where I was a happy, carefree kid. While I'm wise enough to recognize I really can't go home again, I still feel nostalgic out there. It had pleased me to think that Ben McAdams was giving three young girls some of the same memories we had, along with protection from the craziness of the modern world. Walks through woods where the only sounds are birds and whispering trees. Chores that aren't loathsome because animals give affection in return for care. The smell of apple blossoms in the spring, cut hay in the summer, and dry leaves in the fall. Every season and every acre, whether wooded, planted, or pastured, has its own delights. At least, that's how I remember it.

Barb dismissed the topic with a shrug. "She'll get renters. Houses that big are hard to find."

A picture of Mom's house rose in my mind, room after room circling an open space with a narrow stairway at the center. Upstairs, three slanty-roofed bedrooms lined up on the left so that the occupant of the last (Retta, in our case) had had to pass through my room then Barb's to get to the stairway. To the right of the stairs was a large open space, useless except for storage of household castoffs. Rainy days had been perfect for staying inside and going through albums filled with sepia-toned photographs, trunks of old clothes, and other bits of memorabilia every family accumulates.

Outside had been Dad's territory, the barns, the sheds, the fenced pens, and at the edge of the woods, a long, low bunkhouse, occupied in past generations by workers hired during busy times like planting or harvest. These days it was filled with furniture nobody wanted, all of it slowly being eaten away by mice, squirrels, and time.

A thought came to me. "I wonder if Bill might want to move in."

"Bill?" Barb's voice revealed doubt. "Why would he leave Chicago?"

Because he has to, I thought, but I wasn't ready to talk about that yet. Barb has seldom dealt with failure, and I don't think she has any idea what each successive loss does to a person. My son was facing his third failed business, and soon he and his wife would have to move again.

Though Barb obviously thought it was a crazy idea, I wondered if the prospect of moving to Allport might be something they would consider.

Probably not, I told myself firmly. *Bill is a scientist, and Carla is a city girl. No doubt they'd view living in an old house out in the country with the same enthusiasm as being sentenced to ten years in a gulag.*

I sighed. The farm would be rented out to strangers again, and that was probably best.

CHAPTER TWO

Retta

I was still angry with Ben McAdams when I hung up from talking to Faye, but I reminded myself that anger causes wrinkles. At the hallway mirror, I rubbed the spot between my eyes to force the frown away.

The letter lay on the kitchen table, and I read through it again:

> Dear Mrs. Stilson,
> We are all moving to Detroit on Tuesday.
> Thank you for being a nice landlady.
> Sincerly,
> Ben McAdams

Though he'd been my renter for three years, I didn't know a lot about Ben. He always said as little as possible, seldom met my eyes, and slunk away at the earliest opportunity. Once Rose and the girls moved in with him, I don't think Ben ever spoke to me again.

I could see why Rose was attracted to him: dark good looks, a masculine, even macho outlook, and what my novels call a "brooding aspect." Living with such men isn't as romantic as one might imagine, I suspect. Though I liked Rose, I pegged her as the type of woman who's unaware she's allowed a personality and a viewpoint.

I think a lot about women and their views, mostly because my sisters and I see life so differently. Barbara Ann is a pragmatist whose method of dealing with people is to hold most of them at arm's length. She has almost no social life, though in the last year she and the local police chief have become an item. Barbara's really smart when it's something she cares about, but mostly she cares about rules, even dumb ones like when to use who and whom.

Barbara shuts people out; Faye lets everybody in. While Barbara is financially comfortable in her early retirement, Faye had no nest egg and no safety net when she lost her job as an office manager. I think the detective agency is Barbara's way of providing for Faye's old age. Some people think it was an odd choice, but it suits them.

While I don't need a lot of people around me, I don't push them away like Barbara does. Once upon a time I was a perfectly content mother and wife. Then my husband was killed in the line of duty. Don's death was a huge tragedy, but I overcame it with the support of my family and a determination to change things for the better. I spoke all over the state of Michigan about the need to better protect our police officers and even co-wrote a book about it with the help of a young journalist. As a result, I'm pretty well known in Michigan. I have lots of friends, male and female, a healthy bank balance, and an appreciation for nice things and nice people. I'd say my world view is pretty good for a small-town girl who's never been outside the USA.

Returning to the problem of the farm, I took up the phone. Faye had given me the number for a guy named Gabe who, though he'd been a threat in their first case, turned out to be a decent enough person. Not the type you'd trust with national secrets, but fairly honest, fairly ambitious, and kind of sweet.

"This is Gabe." His voice was thin, and I pictured the skinny guy I'd met on the ski trail last winter.

"Hello. It's Margaretta Stilson, of the Smart Detective Agency." I hate even saying that name, but Barbara has so far insisted it will remain. As she pointedly reminds me, the agency is hers and Faye's, not mine.

Gabe's voice brightened considerably when he heard it was me. "Hey, Mrs. Stilson!"

I explained that my tenants had moved, leaving their animals behind. "My sister Faye said you might be willing to go out there mornings for a few days and see to them." I named a generous price, since Faye said Gabe was always in need of cash, being a convicted felon.

"I could use the money," he said, "but I don't know much about animals."

I admitted I didn't either, at least when it came to peafowl and reindeer. Ask me about dogs, and I'll talk all day. "I'm going out there this afternoon. If you meet me, we can look things over and decide if it's something you can do."

"Okay. Where is it?"

From what I knew of Gabe, I guessed he didn't have GPS. "You're going to leave Allport going north, take Taylor Road west for a mile, then turn north again on Pratt until you come to Henning. About a half mile down, there's a long driveway that runs between two wheat fields."

There was a pause. "Can you start again from Taylor Road?" When I didn't answer right away he explained, "Once I been someplace I can find it again easy, but I have trouble with north and west and stuff like that."

Suggesting he write it down, I waited while he dug up a pen and paper. Then I began again, speaking slowly, using landmarks as guides and instructing him to turn right or left rather than using compass points. Once I finished, Gabe read them back to me, and I made a few clarifications. We agreed to meet out there at two.

CHAPTER THREE

Faye

The idea of my two boys living on the farm wouldn't leave my head, no matter how many times I told myself it was just a dream. At lunch I talked with Dale about it, and he surprised me by suggesting I approach Cramer. "You'll just go over and over it in your head until you find out," he said. "If Cramer says no, you'll have to give it up. If he says yes, you can take the next step and ask Bill."

After an injury on a timbering job, Dale is incapacitated in some ways. Despite that, he has a down-to-earth way of looking at a problem and putting his finger on the simplest way to go at it.

Cramer's a computer tech who works pretty much on his own, so I called right away. After I explained my idea, he thought about it for several seconds. "Actually, Mom, that might work for me. I've always loved Grandpa's place, and where I live now doesn't have many good memories. It would be nice to live somewhere else, and cheaper too."

I tried to be objective "You might not think that come winter. The driveway is a half mile long."

"Yeah," he said, "but Bill has the Honda and I've got my truck. We should be okay if we get a plow blade for one of them."

"So you'll actually consider this? I mean, the animals are going to require a lot of care."

"Bill would have to do most of it, but I don't mind helping out on weekends," Cramer said. "If I get my deposit back from here, I could pay Aunt Retta the first two months' rent, which will give them time to figure things out. If the last renters sold eggs and peacock feathers and whatever, they'll have a ready-made customer base, and I could set them up on Etsy or some other site where people sell stuff."

I was almost holding my breath. Was this going to work? The thought of my boys taking over the farm made my chest feel full to bursting. I found myself wishing I could tell Dad. It would have pleased him.

Of course Bill and Carla had no idea of the plans I was making for them. Cramer volunteered to call them and present the idea. "That way, if they really don't want to do it, they won't feel like they're disappointing you." Cramer has a gift for sensing what will make others comfortable and providing it without expecting gratitude or even consideration. His ex-wife was a woman with no capacity for either.

I didn't see that Bill and Carla had much choice, given their present situation. They both love animals, and Carla had grieved deeply a few months back when their Mastiff

13

got hip dysplasia and had to be put down. Crossing my fingers, I hoped peafowl, reindeer, and chickens were also to her liking.

CHAPTER FOUR

Barb

I was out of the office all day, working on a robbery Faye and I were investigating. A midnight break-in had garnered attention from the press and the local police, at least at first. When the leads dried up, the owner asked Allport's police chief, Rory Neuencamp, to recommend someone who could spend more time on the case than his officers could. Rory mentioned the Smart Detective Agency, probably because we have a good reputation for solving cases, but possibly also because he is, for lack of a better term, my boyfriend. He shared what he had on the case with me, admitting they'd done what they could and come up with nothing.

Faye and I were monitoring places we thought the robbers might try to sell the stolen goods. She searched Internet sites while I visited pawn shops in a widening circle—actually more of an arc since Allport lies along the shore of Lake Huron. Everywhere I stopped, I showed photos of the missing items.

My luck had been good. I located several items I was sure were from the robbery, and I even had a photograph of the guy who pawned them, thanks to the store's surveillance camera. Turning the evidence over to Rory's secretary, I went back to the office to report to Faye.

The Smart Detective Agency was Faye's idea, and I had agreed to it mostly because I wanted her to have an income and a job that provided independence from petty bosses. There was also the fact I'd been bored silly after only a few months of retirement.

Faye has always known what I'll be good at better than I do. It was she who told the high school debate coach that her sister would make a great addition to his team. It was Faye who assured me I should skip community college and go directly to the University of Michigan. And it was Faye who insisted I could use the talents I developed in the years I spent as an assistant district attorney to become a successful investigator. As usual, she was right. After a year as a private detective, I couldn't imagine doing anything else.

As I told Faye the details of the afternoon's discoveries, I could see her mind was elsewhere. From her comment about Bill, I thought I knew what was distracting her. Faye's son considers himself an environmental entrepreneur, but nothing he's done in that field has turned out well. After community college, Bill spent several years and lots of investors' money trying to develop a disaster relief communication system, but it never worked as he hoped. Later he invested heavily in generating energy from wave motion in the Great Lakes, but his method proved too expensive to be useful. Most recently he'd formed a cooperative in Chicago, inviting people to live a minimalist lifestyle. It went well at first, but members began abandoning the project when the realities of living without modern conveniences set in. If Faye's long face and lack of updates were an indication, Bill and his wife were stuck with an old apartment building they had taken a year's lease on and a rapidly dwindling list of tenants. I guessed she was about to bail them out. Again.

Faye wanted the farm for Bill and Carla, but I didn't see that working. Retta, an advocate of tough love, would never agree to more than a slight discount for a family member, and she'd require first and last month's rent. Besides, would Bill and his sweet but city-bred wife want to live in a crumbling old house miles from the nearest fast-food restaurant?

"They might," Faye responded when I asked. She continued working as we talked, printing off the paperwork for billing the jewelry store owner.

"And the rent?"

She took out an envelope and stuck an address label on it. "Cramer said he'll take the bunkhouse. With his IT job at the factory and whatever Bill and Carla can contribute, they'll manage until Bill gets something going."

"I take it Justine left again?" Cramer is an overly-loyal type who had allowed his wife to walk over him time and time again. First she left with a man she met on the Internet; she returned because it didn't work out. She left again when Handsome Stranger #2 came along, that time filing for divorce. She came back six months later, sad-eyed and repentant. Cramer, a truly nice guy, ignored the completed divorce proceedings and let her move back in. Cramer isn't stupid, just really, really loyal.

"She took off last week after running up a ton of credit card bills," Faye said, "but if he gives up the apartment, he can pay them off in no time."

I considered. "Retta would agree if they can scrape together the deposit and find homes for the animals."

"I'll pay the deposit." Faye's grin said she couldn't help herself. "And both my boys love critters. They won't mind taking care of them." Peeling a stamp off the roll, she applied it to the envelope. "If they take over the farm, I'll get something I want."

"Which is?"

"Winston Darrow's horses."

An earlier case involved the death of a woman whose husband now had no use for the two animals she'd loved. Faye has always liked horses, but it seemed her feelings were stronger than I guessed. "You aren't going to take up riding again in your fifties!"

"Probably not, but those horses saved my life." Faye set the letter on the pile of outgoing mail. "I've always wanted to adopt retired draft horses. "Do you know how many are put down because no one will take them in?"

"Draft horses. You mean like Clydesdales?"

"That's what a lot of people think when they hear the term, but there are other types: Shires, Percherons, Belgians—" She waved the current envelope to indicate there were others she couldn't name at the moment.

"Like the cart horses on Mackinac Island?"

Situated in the straits between Lake Huron and Lake Michigan, Mackinac Island is known for its ban on automobiles. Horses do the bulk of the work, carrying goods, luggage, and tourists around its 3.8 square miles.

"Right. When they get too old to work they deserve a peaceful old age and people who are good to them. Bill and Carla could be those people."

"What about finances? It costs money to keep horses." I didn't say out loud that Bill had never shown much talent for handling money, but Faye read my mind, as usual.

"Cramer will do the business stuff." She grinned wryly. "He's good with money as long as his ex-wife stays away, and I bet she will once she hears he's living on a farm ten miles from town."

I had to admit, Faye had thought it through. While I wasn't certain it would work out as she hoped, it seemed worth trying. Faye would get her horses, her sons would get a home, and Retta would have one less thing to fuss about.

CHAPTER FIVE

Retta

When I went to meet Gabe at the farm after lunch, I took Styx, my monster-sized Newfoundland, along. He loves to ride in the car, loves exercise, and often serves as my protection. While I'm not afraid of Gabe, being a detective (auxiliary detective to be precise) has made me realize that even the world around Allport can turn threatening. Although he's a real sweetheart, one look at Styx would make someone think twice about robbing me or stealing my car.

As Styx drooled onto a towel I'd placed on the seat, I recalled the agonizingly long bus ride the three of us had endured to get to school each day. I'd hated every minute of it, and once Barbara Ann got her driver's license, I worked to stay on her good side so I never had to ride the Big Banana again. In my opinion, school buses are mobile torture chambers. Barbara and Faye never let anyone harass me, but it was hard, hearing big kids pick on little ones who didn't have older siblings to protect them.

The last four miles of the trip was on gravel roads, which slowed me considerably. I finally turned onto the long driveway we'd once trekked to meet the bus. The fields on either side, farmed by local agri-businessman Chet Masters, are flat and arable. Chet appreciates that; I appreciate the fact that his checks come in like clockwork. Hulking pieces of farm equipment lined the drive, waiting to be used. They might have done their work already. I don't pay much attention to farm stuff.

Parking in front of the house, I let Styx out of the back of my Acadia. He immediately broke into a run, circling the house once before peeing on some bushes. He started around again, this time stopping to sniff the flower beds, the doors, and anything else that caught his interest. Letting him have his fun, I surveyed the yard.

Memories of Mom cling to the house because of the flowerbeds she so lovingly maintained year after year. The peonies were just greenery this early, but daffodils and tulips bobbed in the breeze. Bushes Mom had trimmed and tended would flower throughout the summer. Snowballs, spirea, and lilacs had already begun perfuming the air, and birds chirped overhead, happy for the sunshine.

I paused for a moment, taking in nature's beauty. Then I took out my phone and checked my messages, answering a couple and sending the rest to the trash.

As Styx circled the house yet again, Gabe pulled up in an old pickup with the driver's side door smashed in. To get out, he slid across the bench seat and opened the passenger door. "In February a guy came right through an intersection and hit me," he said as he approached. "I'm saving up to get it fixed." Guessing he had no insurance, I decided to add a bonus if he did the current job well.

Bounding around the house, Styx saw that we had company. He loped forward, skidded to a halt, and set his front paws on Gabe's shoulders in his usual greeting. It was unfortunate, because the dirt he'd picked up from the damp yard left two smeary prints on Gabe's gray jacket.

"Styx, get down!" I ordered, but he paid no attention. Having met Styx before, Gabe gave him the affection he craved, rubbing his sleek head and patting his wide shoulders. When Styx finally backed off, I wiped at Gabe's jacket with a tissue.

"Just dirt, Miz Stilson," he said with a laugh. "It don't hurt a thing."

I warmed a little more toward Gabe. Even if he was clueless about animals, he seemed to have a sense for their needs.

"Let me show you around." I turned to the outbuildings, seeing them as Gabe might. The barn directly ahead of us was well-maintained, though gray with age. It was built into a hill that turned into woods just over the crest. On the bottom level were cattle stalls, above was hay storage. On our left were the sheds and pens: a granary, a corn crib, a chicken coop, and a toolshed. Between those structures and the barn was the yard, fairly dry for late May. I recalled with disgust the way it had looked and smelled when Dad raised cattle. Spring had been the worst, and I recalled being horribly embarrassed once when a boy I liked came to pick me up and made a disgusted face at the smell of the stinky muck.

Along the far sides of the outbuildings were several kinds of animals in crudely partitioned pens. Nearest were half a dozen reindeer, who regarded us with casual interest. Rushing past Gabe and me at a dead run, Styx approached them, barking loudly. Surprisingly, the deer moved forward, curious to meet this new creature.

Styx stopped, confused by the fact that the deer didn't retreat from his ferocious bark. Momentarily at a loss, he spotted a second pen containing peafowl and chickens. Apparently feeling better about this new quarry, he went after them. The chickens scattered, bumping into each other in their hurry to get away. The peafowl retreated unwillingly, with human-like squawks of protest. One female flapped her wings, flying to the top of a fencepost and roosting there in hopes of safety.

Satisfied that he'd made a commotion there, Styx turned to the barnyard, where a bull and two heifers stood along the fence, munching grass. Rolling their eyes, the cows backed away as he went at them in full bark. The bull merely lowered his head as if daring the dog to come closer.

Even a Newfoundland has to respect the territory of an irritable bull. Styx stopped, contenting himself with sounds that asserted his dominance without having to prove it.

Watching Styx entertain the animals, I noticed they'd been fed. There was corn on the ground for the fowl, and the water trough was full.

"Masters must have fed them when he came out this morning," I told Gabe. Farmers are great about helping each other out, knowing there might come a time when they need help.

Gabe and I explored a little, searching out the bags of feed and tools he'd need to see to things.

"If it's okay with you, I'll bring my girlfriend out with me tomorrow," he said. "She knows lots about a lot of animals 'cause of 4-H growing up."

"That sounds good." I had considered calling the local animal shelter and having them come and take the animals, but that would strain their resources. If Gabe and his girlfriend could cope for a few days, Faye would have time to put the plan she proposed into effect. Then the animals would be Bill and Cramer's headache, not mine.

"Let me know if you run into any problems," I said. "I expect to have tenants in a week or so."

"Okay." He looked at the reindeer, who stood at the fence, watching us with interest. "Pretty, ain't they?"

"Yes."

"You go ahead. I'm going to pet them so they get used to me."

Another good sign. Gabe didn't intend to do only what
he had to. He wanted to do it correctly.

"Come on, Styx," I called. Leaving Gabe to his deer-
whispering, I started toward the house with the dog at my
heels. We passed a pile of slab wood, an overgrown stack
of bricks, and an ancient riding lawnmower parked atop
some straw. Styx found the latter interesting and stopped
to investigate.

"Styx, come on." He ignored me. "Styx!"

It took a sharp tug on his pink collar to get him to
follow me. (I like pink, and my dog is very secure in his
masculinity.) I guessed there was a mouse or a mole hiding
under the lawnmower's frame.

Stepping onto the creaky front porch, I let myself in.
Styx left his outside exploring and bumped past me to
investigate the inside smells. I stood for a second in the
narrow doorway, looking around. The house was familiar
in some ways, alien in others. Mother's china closet had
been moved into the living room to make space in the
dining area for Rose's crafts. The top of the dining table
was invisible under stacks of fabric. In one corner was an
old Singer sewing machine, black with age. In another was
a spinning wheel flanked with baskets of yarn. Plank
shelves supported by bricks held stacks of colorful items,
neatly folded.

In addition to the misplaced china closet, the living
room contained two shabby upholstered chairs,
mismatched end tables topped with cheap Christian bric-

a-brac, and rag rugs that were almost certainly home-made. A bookshelf near the doorway was stuffed with aged paperback books, mostly Christian nonfiction and inspirational fiction.

Why had they left so much stuff behind? Didn't they realize someone would have to spend days cleaning up after them? I'd judged Ben and Rose to be odd people. I hadn't guessed they were thoughtless as well.

Near my elbow, a book was shelved sideways atop the others in the row. An oversized piece of paper stuck out of its pages, and I took it out and read it. It was a church bulletin from the River of Fulfilling Life Church on Cable Street in Allport. Turning it over, I saw Ben McAdam listed as one of the church elders.

They'd had a decent house, a self-sufficient lifestyle that apparently suited them, and a support group at church, yet they'd moved away abruptly, leaving most of their stuff behind. Whatever happened must have been either very good, winning the lottery or getting a big inheritance, or very bad. Somehow I doubted Ben McAdams had any rich relatives, and I didn't see him as the type to buy lottery tickets. I guessed the reason they left was something bad.

I had a lot on my plate, but the disappearance of Ben and his family demanded further investigation. Taking my cell from a convenient pocket at one end of my purse, I called Barbara. "Ben McAdams attended the River of Fulfilling Life Church in Allport. I think you should go over there and talk with the pastor to see if he knows where they went."

There was a pause, and I guessed Barbara was thinking something like, *You're not the boss of me.* In an attempt to soothe her ruffled feathers I explained, "I'm supposed to help out at the school with plans for the graduation ceremony. I'm the only one who remembers what has to get done and how to do it."

Barbara still didn't say anything, so I went on. "I've arranged for Gabe to care for the animals." It wasn't as if I wasn't doing my part. "These people left most of their stuff behind, Barbara Ann. We need to make sure there's nothing wrong."

When she finally spoke, her tone said clearly she could have argued but had decided not to. "Do you have an address?"

I supplied the one on the back of the bulletin. "You're the best, Sis."

"Yes," Barbara said. With that she ended the call.

Gabe was still at the corral fence, and one of the reindeer was eating something out of his hand. I tugged at Styx's collar, coaxing him toward the car. He gave the animals a few parting barks before climbing onto his towel-covered seat, sorry to leave such an interesting place but happy to be going anywhere I was going.

CHAPTER SIX

Barb

It isn't that I mind doing things for Retta. It's the way she expects me to do as she says that irritates me. When I told Faye I'd been ordered to visit the church McAdams attended, she played peacemaker, offering to go. "That isn't the point," I told her. "The question is why doesn't Retta do it? Apparently it's something about graduation."

Faye chuckled. "Last year someone decided that instead of blue and gold flowers for graduation, they'd have blue and gold and white. Retta almost had a fit. Nobody changes tradition if she can prevent it."

I sighed. "Okay, so while Retta saves Allport High from eternal embarrassment, I get to interview a man I don't know about a family I never met concerning an emergency that probably never happened."

Faye grinned. "Good luck with that."

The church was a modular building in a mostly residential neighborhood. There were chairs instead of pews, narrow windows with regular glass, and a slightly rickety-looking speaker's platform up front made of particle board covered with wafer-thin, fake wood paneling. The pastor, a slightly round young man with Buddy Holly glasses, greeted me politely when I tapped on the door of his office.

"Aaron Cronk," he said, shaking my hand. "What can I do for you?"

He frowned as I explained the McAdams family's move. "I didn't know they were leaving," he said, "but that's no surprise."

"What do you mean?"

"Ben doesn't trust many people, and he often doesn't share his plans." A moment later he added, "I guess it's good they left as a family."

"Meaning you thought Ben and the woman might split?" Though I'd tried to recall her name on the way over, I couldn't. Retta had mentioned it more than once, but I often don't listen when she goes into one of her stories about people I don't know and don't need to.

Cronk shifted his feet. "It isn't my place to tell tales."

"Mr. Cronk, we'd like to return the family's possessions to them. That means we need to know where they are. If the woman and McAdams went separate ways, it would be helpful to know that." Gathering bits of memory I said, "Ben rented the farm as a single man, right? The woman and her daughters joined him later."

He nodded. "When Rose's husband died in an accident, she tried to make a go of a yarn shop. Though she's a talented artist, she couldn't handle the business

29

part. Ben, a strong church member, lived all alone in that big house." He clasped his hands as if it were natural for a single female to join with the first unattached male who came along. "Rose came to me for counsel, and I encouraged her to accept Ben's offer of protection."

"Moving in with McAdams gave her financial security." I'd have suggested a college business course, but I kept that opinion to myself.

"I thought they'd marry. Rose said she wasn't sure she cared for Ben in the way a wife should for her husband." His hands fluttered to demonstrate how helpless he'd felt at her decision. "I hoped she'd come to her senses in time, but I'm afraid things got worse between them." He shook his head. "Rose couldn't see that Ben was God's match for her."

A preacher who spouted commercial taglines? If Rose refused to marry Ben, she'd probably had her reasons. Judging from Retta's reports that Rose and the girls had always been busy tending, making, and fixing, it seemed that McAdams had benefited as much as the woman he offered his "protection" to.

"You said you aren't surprised they left. Why's that?"

Again the pastor paused, reluctant to share what he knew. "They'd become less involved in the church lately." He rubbed his chin. "I've been meaning to go out there for a month, but something always came up. You're sure they're gone?" He seemed embarrassed, and I wondered if he suspected Ben wasn't as good to Rose as he should have been.

"They sent my sister a letter," I said. "It said they were moving to Detroit."

He looked up sharply. "I don't think so."

I shrugged. "That's what the note said."

He chewed on his bottom lip for a while. "I can't imagine Ben moving there." He leaned in as if confiding a secret. "It's full of Mohammedans."

"Mo—You mean Muslims?"

"Yes." Cronk shook his head, making his jowls shudder. "I don't think he'd expose his family to those people."

"I see." Irritated by the man's blanket prejudice, I took out a business card. "If you hear from Rose or Ben, please ask them to contact me or my sister." I wrote Retta's cell number on the back.

Cronk studied the card with interest. "Are you the lady who caught those killers last winter?"

"My sister and I helped out with the case." I didn't say we got involved because the man accused of murdering his wife had been Retta's boyfriend. We'd been relieved when it turned out he hadn't committed murder on her behalf.

"A detective agency, eh?" The way he said it implied that our offices would be located between a bar and a brothel. Still, he set my card carefully on his desk and wished me a blessed day.

CHAPTER SEVEN

Faye

I was in my car Wednesday morning when the phone rang. Pulling into a nearby parking lot, I took the call.

"Good morning, Mom. Are you busy?"

"Hi, Bill. I'm on my way to the Meadows, either to rescue your grandmother from something or to rescue the staff from your grandmother. There's no hurry, though. How are you, Sweetie?"

"We're good—actually, really good after Cramer's call last night."

My heart gave a little skip. "You like my idea?"

"It couldn't have come at a better time for us."

That meant things were getting down to the wire. "So tell me what you think should happen, and I'll try to help."

"Well, Carla and I thought we'd drive up this weekend and see the place. I mean, I remember it from when I was a kid, but it's been a while. Once we know what's there, we'll rent a truck and make the move." He cleared his throat before adding, "We'd like to be out of here by June first."

Ten days. Rent was no doubt due at the first of the new month.

"I think we can do that. I talked to Retta, and she's happy to get someone to take on the animals. She's looking for the previous renters so we can make them take their stuff, but if she can't locate them, we'll dispose of it later."

"We don't have that much to bring."

I heard tension in Bill's voice and felt a pang of sadness. He was so smart, so good! He'd just never found the right way to use his talents. I said a little prayer this would be his answer.

That made me think of my daughter-in-law. "Is Carla okay with this?"

He chuckled. "I think she's more excited than I am. She's filled sheets of paper with diagrams of garden plots." He lowered his voice. "I'm hoping this will take her mind off the other thing, you know?"

"I know." Carla had recently had her third miscarriage in four years. Their childless marriage had begun worrying her, and her worry made Bill sad.

"Okay," I said, turning to a happier subject. "I'm going to call Retta right now, and I'll see you in a few days."

"Right. And Mom," Bill's voice turned soft. "Thanks so much for this. We're going to make it work. I promise."

"Good." No one knew if my sons could pull off my crazy scheme, but the fact they were willing to try meant a lot to me.

CHAPTER EIGHT

Barb

A few minutes after Faye left for the nursing home, I heard the front door open. We operate our agency out of my home, so far with no complaints from the neighbors. The rambling old Victorian had two parlors at the front when I moved in, one formal and the other less so. After we re-varnished the wide, dark woodwork and applied cream-colored paint to the walls, the parlors became our business space.

I stepped out of my office, the former second parlor, to see who was there. Standing in the reception area was a thirtyish man with dark, curly hair and the kind of face that will never look old. "Good day, ma'am."

I stepped forward, holding out a hand. "Barb Evans, half of the agency."

His handshake was brief. "Colt Farrell. I think you ladies might be able to help me find some people." Something in his tone hinted he was favoring our business with his presence, but I smiled, withholding judgment.

"Come in, Mr. Farrell." I led him into my office, glancing around to reassure myself it was as I like it. If I'm not vigilant, Retta adds touches to my space that she thinks add style and color. She favors Southwest decor, and early on it was cactus plants and desert paintings. I'd explained to her that while I have nothing against the Southwest, I don't want it in my stately Victorian home.

I invited my guest to be seated then asked, "Whom do you want to locate, Mr. Farrell?"

"Some friends who left the area. I'm hoping you can give me their forwarding address."

I folded my hands on the desktop. "Why do you want to locate them?" While clients don't always tell the truth about their motives, it's best to ask straight out. When we can avoid it, we refuse to take a case if the client's reasons for wanting our services are frivolous or spiteful.

Farrell made a vague gesture. "I thought we were friends. I mean, Ben and me were friends. I knew Rose and the girls, of course, but—"

The name caught my attention. "You're speaking of Ben McAdams?"

"Yes. I understand you own the farm him and his family were renting." He repeated the gesture, and I thought it signaled frustration. "I didn't think Ben would move away without letting me know where he was going."

"Was there any indication of trouble between the two of them?"

He shrugged. "Ben thought everything was fine."

"What about finances? Did they have money problems?"

"I think they were doing pretty good, better together than either one ever done by themselves."

Trying to ignore the man's grammatical messes, I focused on his purpose. "We don't share information, but I can say we don't know where they are."

Farrell rubbed one side of his face. "I just don't understand it." He glared at the items on my desk as if Ben might be hiding behind one of them. "I hope none of them got sick or something. Not a week ago I was out to the house, and he never said a thing about moving away."

There was something false in Farrell's voice. It occurred to me that McAdams probably owed Farrell money. He didn't seem angry about it, however, just disbelieving.

I opened my mouth to say that if we located the family, we'd ask McAdams to contact him. Farrell picked up a cup of pencils sitting on my desk, and he read aloud Clare Boothe Luce's words: "If I fail, no one will say, 'She doesn't have what it takes.' They will say, 'Women don't have what it takes.'"

He frowned. "Did this Clare have what it takes?"

"She was a writer, an ambassador, successful at a lot of things."

"And what did her husband do for a living?"

His tone was like a poke in my side with a stick. "Why do you ask?"

Farrell shrugged lightly. "I notice that a lot of successful women have wealthy husbands that support them so they can write books and go to ambassador balls and like that."

My lips were stiff as I replied, "I don't."

He seemed confused. "You mean you don't have a successful husband?"

"I don't have any husband, Mr. Farrell. Never have."

His jaw jutted. "Now, that's sad."

"I don't find it so."

He looked as if he pitied me. "Then you don't understand God's plan. For a woman, the purpose of life is marriage and children."

I leaned back in my chair, possibly so my fist couldn't reach his chin. "And what's the purpose of life for a man?"

He sighed at the weight of the question. "A man has lots of things he's meant to do, but an important one is taking care of his woman." He set the cup back on my desk. "I'm sorry you missed that in your life."

I stood abruptly. "I'm afraid we can't help you, Mr. Farrell."

He rose, brushing his black polyester trousers. "Ben will contact me once they get settled. Thanks for your time, Miss Evans."

As he left, I didn't know whether to laugh or throw something at the back of his head. His parting shot, the use of *Miss*, was a pointed reminder that I exist in a state he believed to be unnatural for women. I guess I should

Maggie Pill

have been grateful he didn't address me as "Spinster Evans."

38

CHAPTER NINE

Faye

I spent an hour with Dale's mom, listening and sympathizing until she talked herself into admitting she really did need help to get out of bed. Though she'd failed in the last few months, Harriet's sense of independence and modesty remained strong. There were days when she got feisty and tried to do for herself, as she had for many years. This time she'd fallen trying to get to the bathroom. She wasn't hurt, but she insisted, "If they'll just give me a cane, "I can pee without some nurse watching!"

The staff at the Meadows had called me to see if I could make Harriet see reason. Though she never liked me much, my mother-in-law had come to see me as an ally in her battle for independence. Everyone in the nursing home wanted her to do things they hoped would keep her alive. While I'm not a big cheerleader for death, I agree with Harriet that dying isn't the worst thing that can happen to a person after ninety.

When I returned to the office, Barb was slumped toward the computer in a very un-ergonomic position.

After she caught me up on Farrell's visit she asked, "Was this Ben McAdams as pompous as his buddy Farrell?"

"I never met him, but Retta can tell us." I called her, putting the phone on speaker.

"I really don't know," Retta said. "Ben didn't talk much, and he never offered an opinion on anything. I don't know if I intimidated him or it was just his natural way. Rose was much easier to deal with."

"The pastor didn't know McAdams was moving and neither did his buddy," Barb said. "Retta, do you think they were running away from something, a debt or a legal problem?"

Retta chuckled. "I don't suppose they'd tell their landlord if they had trouble like that."

"Barb's going to see what she can find out from Rory," I told Retta. Barb was already calling the city police department. Listening in on their conversation, I gathered the chief wasn't overly busy and would check their databases for warrants and watches. After a few minutes of silence I heard Barb say, "No legal issues. Thanks, Rory. I owe you one."

He said something that made her blush, but she simply thanked him again and hung up. "No record of law-breaking for either Ben McAdams or Rose Isley. Ben had some trouble as a kid, went through the foster care system and the juvenile courts, but he joined the military and apparently straightened himself out. No recent events that would explain them moving away abruptly."

I turned the phone toward me. "I'll try the school. The elementary secretary knows me pretty well, and she'll know if there was something going on, even if she can't tell us exactly what it was."

It took a few minutes to connect, and I pictured the busy office with teachers, parents, kids, and staff all making demands on the secretary's time. Even after twenty years on the job, Madge never failed to be patient with everything and kind to everyone.

When Madge finally answered I got right to the point, knowing she didn't have time for idle chatter. "I'm calling about the Isley children. I think two of them are in elementary. Did they tell you they were moving away?"

"No, but we wondered. They withdrew from school about a month ago."

"Why?"

"Ben said they'd decided to homeschool, but April is a funny time to start that. They'd be smarter to start in the fall."

"Did anyone talk to the girls' mother to see if she agreed with Ben?"

Madge chuckled. "Mrs. White tried, but you don't just call out there. Ben is kind of a Luddite, so Rose and the girls don't have phones or computers. He has a cell phone, but he turns it off most of the time. You have to leave a voicemail, and he answers if and when he feels like it."

"Hard to believe in this day and age."

"Inconvenient, if you ask me." She sniffed. "You say they're moving?"

"Retta got a letter saying they were, so she went out there. They're already gone." Not wanting to start rumors I added, "We were surprised, but we have no reason to believe there's anything wrong."

"Hmmm," Madge seemed skeptical. "I'll ask the kids who are friends with Pansy and Daisy." After a beat she added, "And I'll check with the middle school secretary. Iris might have said something to one of her friends."

"Thanks, Madge."

Barb had been checking computer records as I talked, an ever-present tissue crumpled in one hand. People with sinus problems probably shouldn't live in century-old houses. "I can't find credit card accounts under either Rose's name or Ben's," she said when I ended my call.

"I think we're dealing with a guy who won't have credit cards," I told her, "maybe not even a bank account. Retta says the rent came by money order, sometimes in cash."

"Is he a survivalist or something?"

"I guess he'd call himself an individualist."

"What about the woman? Did she go along with it?"

"She must have." A hot flash hit and I stripped off my sweater. Barb gripes about her drippy sinuses, but she's never had a single hot flash, so I contend she's the lucky one. "Ben isn't Rose's husband. He has no say over her or the girls."

"True." Barb tossed her tissue and picked up another. "But with three daughters and no money, she might not have had anywhere else to go."

CHAPTER TEN

Retta

On Wednesday afternoon I went back out to the farm. Faye had talked her boys into moving out there, and I wanted to make sure the bunkhouse was suitable for habitation. Faye's proposal was that Cramer, Bill, and Carla would take a year's lease on the place. The deal was that Bill would take over the farmhouse with his wife Carla, and Cramer would move into the bunkhouse. They'd take care of the animals until we decided what to do with them. In addition they agreed to move the previous tenants' stuff upstairs until we located them or disposed of it some other way. For me, Faye's idea meant a lot less headaches.

On the other hand, I don't have much faith in Faye's two younger sons. They're nice boys, but neither Cramer nor Bill seems able to get control of his life. Bill is always hatching some half-baked scheme, and Cramer has let that wife of his—ex-wife now—lead him around by the nose for almost a decade. I wanted to believe they'd be good tenants and good animal tenders as well, but I try to practice logic like a good detective should. With that in mind, I was withholding judgment.

Aside from being dusty, crowded, and full of cobwebs, the bunkhouse looked okay. It was no palace, but honestly, all Cramer wants is lots of electrical plugs for the computer equipment he collects. Looking at the rather stark interior, I decided to buy some colorful curtains and throw rugs. He probably wouldn't notice, but it would make me feel better.

The thought of decorating Cramer's space reminded me of Barbara Ann's need for an artist's touch. Faye was preoccupied with her sons, and Barbara planned to go out of town for the weekend. It was the perfect time for me to spruce up her office.

Everyone says I'm the artistic one in the family, but my sisters didn't consult me when they started their business. Faye's office, which is also the entry area, isn't too bad. She's created ambiance with a half-dozen plants and scattered displays of glass figurines she collected over the years. Some of them were our grandmother's, and they're really quite beautiful.

Barbara's office, on the other hand, is as cold as Superman's Fortress of Solitude. You'd think an antique wooden desk and rows of books would result in a comfortable atmosphere, but there isn't a single decorative item to add interest. The light walls and dark woodwork cry out for accent colors, and there's almost no fabric to soften the perpendicular lines: no curtains, no pillows, nothing that doesn't serve a business purpose. Once I suggested she do a wall montage with some of her pictures and awards from Tacoma, but she said that was all in the past. Past or not, visitors would be impressed to see Barbara Ann pictured with a senator and the former vice president.

Though I had my eye out for just the right things, so far I hadn't found them. There was no doubt I'd find just what she needed, and Barbara would get some unexpected gifts. I love buying things for people!

When Styx and I got to the farm, I was pleased to see the animals had fresh food and water. Gabe and his girlfriend must be early risers.

Styx had already lost interest in chasing chickens and cattle, and while I wandered around looking into various bins and barns, he returned to sniffing at the lawnmower he found so interesting the day before.

I let myself into the house, less overwhelmed by the clutter since there'd soon be someone here to remove it. I wandered through the rooms, looking idly at what my renters had deemed too unimportant to take with them. In the corner of the dining room was a battered roll-top desk that had been our father's business center. Raising the roller, I found stacks of paper: full-size sheets, notepads from feed stores, and scraps torn from old letters and envelopes. Rose's filing system wasn't organized, but there were notes on what she'd earned at craft shows, and what they'd made from the sale of farm goods: eggs, milk, and the occasional whole animal.

I sifted through the papers, not looking for anything in particular. It occurred to me there wasn't any sort of tax information, no large envelopes numbered with the year of filing, no forms or bundled receipts. None of the stuff the IRS says you're supposed to keep for five years or seven years or forever.

On the floor beside the desk sat an ancient electric typewriter, probably a cast off from some office or school. The letter I received from McAdams had been typed, with strike-overs and uneven ink. I wondered where Rose had found ribbons for that old dinosaur.

Wandering into what had been my parents' bedroom, I took a few minutes to strip the sheets off the bed. Faye and Dale planned to spend a night at the farm to get things ready for her two horses and her two boys, and it wasn't right for them to have to sleep in someone else's bed linens. Digging around in the closet, I found paper-thin but clean sheets and mismatched pillowcases. I'd have aired the mattress if time permitted, but I was able to locate an ancient Electrolux and give everything a thorough vacuuming before putting on fresh bedding.

On the bedside table was a Bible, and I picked it up and flipped through its pages. Passages were marked with slips of paper, and masculine handwriting noted specific verses, apparently ones Ben was taken with. I read two,

Ephesians 5:22-27 and 1 Peter 3:1-5. Both were passages ordering women to accept their husbands' will.

Was that why Rose had refused to marry Ben? If she remained single, was she exempt from the Biblical direction that wives "submit to your husbands"? She'd been under Ben's thumb either way, as far as I could tell. No matter what Rose believed, Ben called the shots.

At the back of Ben's Bible were several folded sheets of paper. Taking them out, I skimmed the very un-Biblical material. It was from the Internet, which meant Ben had gotten it somewhere besides here. Called "Living off the Grid," it listed ways to avoid the notice of governmental agencies, federal, state, and local. Readers were advised to buy their guns from private owners, use the Internet only at public sites like libraries, and limit interaction with entities that store personal information.

I shivered as I put the pages back into the Bible and dumped it into the night stand drawer. Ben was creepier than I originally thought, and I was glad he no longer slept in my parents' bed.

CHAPTER ELEVEN

Barb

I woke in the night to a metallic pecking outside my window. Glancing at the clock—3:00 a.m.—I frowned at the closed blind. A second-story man? Doubtful. A curious bird? I waited. The sound intensified. Something was trying to break through the screen.

Taking up the flashlight from my nightstand, I swung it a few times to test its aptitude as a weapon. Solid, and it fit nicely in my hand. Leaving my bed, I crept softly across the room and put my back to the wall beside the window. Slowly, I drew the curtain aside.

At first I saw nothing unusual. My side yard was partially lit by a street lamp some distance away. The porch roof was a foot below me, and a large old maple tree spread its branches toward it, a few of its leaves resting on the shingles. Nothing moved. It wasn't a branch scraping across the roof.

Dropping the curtain, I moved softly to the other side of the window and looked out. There was almost no light there, but I saw a flash of movement. Something grated against the screen, stopped, and grated again. This time I saw the noise-making implement.

A cat's claw.

Leaning forward, I aimed the light at the animal and turned it on. Yellow eyes reflected the light back at me for a second before it turned and ran down the porch roof. It was a gray tabby, long in the body and narrow at the hips. Perfect for sliding through alleys and squeezing through fences. In no time the animal was out of sight.

I listened, but the cat was as silent as she was quick. Clicking off the flashlight, I smiled to myself. A kitty ninja, attacking then disappearing without a trace.

I watched the dark street for a while, identifying with the cat. Like her, I sometimes go out on my own at night, not to force my way into people's homes, but to fix grammatical and spelling errors on signs in the Allport area. Because of my own ninja activities, I know what it's like to skulk in the shadows and bolt for safety when there's danger of discovery.

With a lot on my mind, I doubted I could go back to sleep. Turning on a light, I sat down at my desk and took out the list of corrections I hoped to make over the summer. Over the past year and a half I'd fixed the most egregious errors in signs around town. After I wrote several anonymous letters cautioning the local news team about their grammar, they began correcting themselves, sometimes mid-sentence, aligning their subjects with their verbs and their pronouns with their antecedents.

There was always more to do. A new sweet shop was about to open on Main Street, and I had to look away every time I passed on my morning walks. The sign in the window said, COMMING SOON! GREAT SNACKS AND DESERTS! While that sign would go away once the store opened, I foresaw future problems at that location.

It was my weekly date for a home-cooked breakfast with Faye and Dale, and I came downstairs at 7:00 to the smell of bacon. Dale stood next to Faye as she mixed batter for French toast. He held a bottle of vanilla, and when she paused, he passed it to her. Setting down the bowl, Faye took the vanilla, murmuring, "Thanks, Hon." They're so cute together.

As she fried the bread to golden brown, Faye caught me up on news about the farm. "Bill and Carla are coming on Saturday, and Cramer already told his landlord he's moving out. Gabe's seeing to the animals until the boys get there to take over."

Taking the toast from the griddle, Faye put it on a plate which she set at the center of the table before sitting down with Dale and me.

I took some bacon and a piece of French toast. "Gabe has experience with reindeer?"

"No, but I guess the girlfriend does." When Faye took a piece for herself, Dale set the butter, syrup, and bacon near her elbow, where she could easily reach them. With a man that attentive, it's no wonder she's put on a few pounds over the years.

When breakfast was finished and Dale went out to his workshop in the back yard, Faye and I settled at our desks. "Any leads on McAdams or Rose from your sources?"

"None." She frowned at the computer screen. "I've tried everything I can think of."

"What are they driving?"

She shrugged. "They have an old extended-cab pickup that's registered in Rose's name. None of my guys have seen it on the road." Faye once had a job in a small factory, where she got to know a lot of truckers. They like her, and from time to time she asks for favors such as watching for certain vehicles on the road. It's surprisingly effective.

"Maybe they left some other way, like by bus." It wasn't logical, but nothing about the situation was. McAdams wasn't in trouble with the law, though he was definitely leery of it. He hadn't told anyone he was moving away, yet they were gone, leaving most of their belongings behind. It was possible they'd left their vehicle behind too.

Faye picked up the phone. "Let's ask Gabe if he's seen the truck out there." Faye called, putting the speaker on so I could hear Gabe's answer.

"I guess it could be down in the woods," he said. "But how would they get where they're going without it?"

"I don't know," Faye said, "but no one's seen it on the road."

"Mindy says this Ben guy was breaking the law. His reindeer haven't got any ear tags, which means the DNR doesn't know they're out here."

"Ear tags?"

"Yeah. You're supposed to tell the DNR and pay a fee if you own reindeer. They come out and inspect them all the time to make sure they don't pick up diseases from the white-tail deer around here."

"Oh." Faye glanced at me. Another indication that McAdams had been leery of letting the government know what he was doing.

"There's something else that's funny," Gabe said. "Somebody fed all the animals again this morning. Your sister thought it was the guy that rents the land, but he just got here. He says he didn't do it either day."

Faye thanked him, hung up, and leaned back in her chair. "It's like the fairy tale where elves come at night and do their work unseen."

"Maybe one of their friends knows the family left and is helping out."

Leaning forward again, Faye checked our appointment book. "My horses are going to be trailered out there this morning, and I want to be there to get them settled. I'll come back here for our meeting at three then after supper, Dale and I will go out and spend the night." She smiled. "I need to be sure the new kids on the farm are okay."

"I'll ride out there with you," I said. "I'd like to see the old place."

Buddy, Faye's dog, entered the office at that moment, and to my dismay she asked, "Do you want to go for a ride, Bud? Want to ride in the car?"

She always talks to him like he understands, and to be fair, the dance he started did seem to indicate he knew the word car.

I don't care much for Buddy, and he returns the sentiment. When Faye found him hurt on the road and brought him home, she was already half in love with him. I'd gulped and agreed he could stay, secretly hoping an owner would show up and claim him. It didn't happen. Since then I've learned it's wise to keep my footwear upstairs unless I want it to look like it's been through a food processor. Buddy stays downstairs, and when he comes to the office, he naps under Faye's desk. I don't snarl back when he snarls at me, and he grudgingly allows me to live in my own home.

We took Faye's car—no way was I letting that dog ride in mine—and Buddy stayed in the back seat, which was a miracle. He usually rides in front, and I knew his coarse hairs would attach themselves to my clothing. When we got to the farm and Faye opened the back door to let him out, I noticed the leg broken when Buddy was hit by a car last winter had healed nicely. Showing no sign of pain or stiffness, the dog headed immediately to a lawn mower parked at the front of the house. He whined a little, and Faye went over to see what he'd found.

"What is it, Bud?" She walked all the way around the mower, but there was nothing there. Apart from the fact that it was parked in an odd place, it was just an old piece of lawn equipment. Buddy seemed anxious, whining and digging at the tires. Faye asked him several times what was wrong, like he was going to tell her in plain English. In the end we walked away, leaving him to his doggie oddness.

I hadn't been to the farm in years, but it wasn't much different. Faye led the way into the large barnyard through the smaller of two gates, dropping a leather strap over the gatepost to keep the larger animals in. The reindeer saw us coming and approached, not cowed in the least by two strange women and a dog. One stuck its nose right over the fence and tried to explore my jacket pocket, apparently looking for treats. I moved back to avoid it, but Faye let the animal nudge her, leaving a wet stain on her shirt. "Let's see what's available for horse feed," she said.

The cattle were out, and the two cows looked over their shoulders at us with that bored expression they all seem to cultivate. The bull regarded us with belligerence when I opened the gate, but taking up a shovel that leaned against the gatepost, Faye brandished it at him. The bull backed away, choosing discretion for the time being.

Watching where we stepped, we circled the barnyard. The animals had indeed been fed recently. There was a shiny new salt block at one corner of the barnyard, and the stable had been mucked out fairly recently. "Somebody's watching out for these critters," Faye said. "Neighbors?"

"The nearest neighbors can't even see this place. How would they know the tenants are gone?"

"Maybe Ben or Rose asked someone to look in on them." We'd come full circle, and Faye gestured toward the house. "Let's look around inside."

She had some difficulty convincing Buddy to come with us, but he finally left the lawnmower and followed us up the front steps.

It felt odd to enter our parents' house and find it adapted to someone else's liking. I poked around the living room while Faye walked through, cataloging in her mind what Bill and Carla would have to do to make it theirs. As I passed a window, movement out by the barn caught my eye. "There's someone out there."

Faye hurried over to look. "I don't see anybody."

"It was just a flash, but it wasn't an animal. There was pink."

We went back outside, shading our eyes with our hands as we stared at the spot. "Whoever it was went from the hayloft into the woods behind it. It wasn't very big, not a man, I'm pretty sure."

"Neighbor kids?" Faye asked.

"Aren't they still in school?"

"They should be. I heard from Madge last night after you went upstairs. Nobody at the school knows why the Isley girls left and as far as she can learn, the girls never contacted any of their friends once they withdrew."

"You don't suppose McAdams murdered them and took off, do you?"

"If he did, it was very recently. Madge said one of the teachers buys eggs from them, and she saw the girls last weekend."

We'd walked up the hill to where double doors on the west end of the barn allowed entry to the hayloft. I stayed close to Faye, since the bull was once again eyeing us and she had the shovel.

The door was ajar, though we had closed it when we left earlier. The hayloft looked much the same as it had when we were kids, a large space with double doors at the opposite end for loading bales for storage, and a trapdoor in the center for dropping them down to the animals as needed. It was almost empty at this time of year, since the animals needed less hay now that there was tasty green grass to eat.

We stood looking around, seeing nothing unusual and hearing only the ticks of the tin roof as the sun warmed it, expanding the metal. Even Buddy found nothing exciting. He marked the loft for his territory then returned to Faye's side. As we turned to go, a glint caught my eye, and I stooped to see what it was. I picked up a barrette, pink with a single rhinestone at one end, and showed it to Faye.

"Could it be one of Rose's children?" she asked. "What would she be doing here alone?"

"I don't know," I replied, "but I think we need to find out."

Turning to face each other, we said it at the same time. "The cabin."

The original structure on our property is a log cabin built long before our father was born. Over the years, it had fallen into disrepair. Its chinking dried out and fell to the ground. Its door swelled from moisture and stuck shut. The windows no longer had glass, and to be truthful, Faye and I and a BB gun might have had something to do with that. Open to the weather, the cabin became the domain of small animals and dead leaves.

From time to time someone fixed it up a little. As girls we did hours of work cleaning it out so we could sleep there. The plank floor was hard and damp, but the spirit of adventure kept things interesting. Faye's sons had in their turn discovered it, again clearing away years of detritus and using the cabin for camping adventures and possibly a few drinking parties. When they were grown it was forgotten again, so isolated we seldom thought of it.

If someone wanted to hide out on the farm, that was where he'd go.

"Put the dog in the car," I told Faye. "We need to move quietly."

She did as I suggested. Buddy didn't like it, but he's smart enough to sense the times Faye can't be coaxed into changing her mind. Turning around once on the back seat, he settled his nose on his paws and closed his eyes. Taking up her shovel Faye led the way up the hill again, this time passing the barn and heading into the woods.

CHAPTER TWELVE

Faye

Barb and I were quiet, side-stepping twigs and branches that might snap and signal our approach. The cabin sat beside a pond that was sometimes there, sometimes not, depending on the season and the amount of rain. It wasn't far, perhaps half a mile, though as kids we thought the place as remote as Jupiter. Images rose in my mind of the two of us lumbering through the woods weighed down by old blankets, flashlights, crackers, and a half-jar of peanut butter. The last time I recalled making the trip, Retta had insisted she was big enough to go along. Not having the heart to refuse her, Mom had suggested in the strongest terms that we take Baby Sister along. I can still recall Barb's disgust when Retta got scared sometime after midnight and started crying to go home. I'll admit I wasn't thrilled myself as we fumbled our way through the dark woods with her sobbing between us.

We neared the cabin, puffing a lot more than we had as kids, and stopped to catch our breath. Looking down the slight incline, I saw that the pond was fairly big from the rainy April we'd had. The sun lit the water, hiding its murky underside with reflected sparkle. As girls Barb and I tried several homemade watercraft on that muddy mess, the most successful an old door we made into a raft. We had to stand on opposite ends, and our feet had always become soaked, but when we poled like mad and arrived at the opposite shore, we felt like we'd discovered land untouched by other humans.

We moved forward again, keeping trees between us and the door and craning our necks to peer between the newly-sprung leaves. Someone had replaced the broken windows with plastic glass, and the door sat properly in place. At first we saw no sign of life, but then someone passed the window. It was a girl of perhaps twelve, her blond hair bright in the dark space. As we watched, she reappeared, stopping at the window but facing away. Barb touched my arm, and we moved closer.

We reached the cabin wall without making any noise, stopped next to the front window and listened. "You can't go back again," a voice said. "They'll catch us."

"But what about Mazie?" It was clearly the voice of a young child.

"They're going to take care of her from now on. Mazie will be fine."

"But she'll miss us. She wants me and Pansy to feed her!"

Someone sighed in frustration, and another voice chimed in. "Iris is right. We'll get split up and you'll never see me or her again!"

"Pansy, don't," the first one said. "You'll scare her."

The warning came too late. An unintelligible wail rose, ending in a few words we could decipher: "—want to stay with you!"

The pain in that voice was too much. Pushing the door open, I entered the cabin. Three young girls turned to stare at me, their expressions horrified, as if I'd brought poisoned apples for everyone.

Standing so close, they looked like a photo montage of a single child's growing years. All three had honey-colored hair and round, blue-eyes, now shadowed by fear and distrust. Their fair complexions hinted at Nordic heritage, but several days in the woods had dulled them, as if they stood behind old glass.

Wearing a cotton skirt and a faded top, the oldest girl was at the stage writers call coltish. She'd apparently had a growth spurt, because her shirt pinched at the shoulders and the hem of her denim skirt had been let down, revealing a darker color. Her hair was neatly braided into one plait and fastened with limp ribbon. Twelve going on thirty-five.

The middle girl, a stair-step down in height, wore a skirt and top every bit as dull as her sisters'. Her hair was unbound and uncombed, and she'd stuck a screwdriver in her waistband, a nine-year-old's means of defense.

The littlest girl had the round cheeks that are often the last vestiges of baby fat. On one side of her head, a barrette kept her light hair away from her face. It was a mate to the one we'd found in the barn.

Though they appeared to be healthy, none of them was old enough to be living in the woods alone.

Barb spoke calmly from behind me. "Don't be afraid. We want to help."

The oldest girl squared her shoulders, ready to face whatever she had to. The little one stepped behind her sisters, crying softly. I moved toward her, intending to offer comfort, but the middle girl blocked my way, her jaw tight. "Stay away from her!"

"Stop it, Pansy." The oldest girl bent to comfort the little one. "There's nothing we can do now."

I glanced around the one-room cabin. The only furniture was a sturdy bunk bed in the corner away from the window. On each bed a couple of quilts lay neatly folded. In another corner was a cooler, and atop it were ready-to-eat foods: a jar of peanut butter, a stack of crackers, a box of raisins, and a bag of walnuts, along with three cups, three plates, and three sets of silverware. Next to the cooler was a thermal picnic jug.

At the foot of the bed was a large black garbage bag, and spilling from it was an assortment of clothing. Half-covered by the bag's edge was a doll that looked hand-made. Its skirt was the same fabric as the skirt the smallest girl wore, and I pictured Rose making it for her youngest child.

"You're the Isley girls," Barb said.

The oldest girl answered. "I'm Iris. That's Pansy, and Daisy."

"Flowers," I murmured, and she shrugged as if to say it was beyond her why her mother had chosen such names.

"What are you doing out here?"

Daisy looked up, her face wet with tears. "Don't let So-Servishes take us away!" she begged. "I want to live with Pansy and Iris!"

We turned to Iris for a translation. "Ben said the social services people will separate us. We decided to live out here so we could stay together."

"But where are your parents?" Barb's tone indicated disgust with adults who would go away without making arrangements for their children.

More tacit communication. "We don't know." Pansy said as she stroked Daisy's arm. "They just left."

CHAPTER THIRTEEN

Barb

I'm not sure what I expected to find in the woods on our family farm that day, but three unchaperoned children wasn't it. What were we supposed to do with them?

Faye suggested we go back to the farmhouse, where she promised to fix the girls a meal. Food is Faye's way of making everyone comfortable, and it worked. The oldest and youngest of the girls seemed relieved to see their adventure come to an end, and both of them ceded responsibility to the adults without objection.

The middle one, Pansy, had a little more fight in her.

"You aren't the boss of us!" she said when Faye made her proposal. "Our rent is paid until the first of June, so if we want to stay out here, we can."

Faye looked at me with a question in her eyes. "That's not precisely true," I said in my best barrister voice. "The rental contract is with your parents, who aren't here."

She wasn't ready to give up yet. "Well, you aren't our parents, so we don't have to do what you say."

Despite my irritation at having to argue with a child, I admired the girl's active mind. "You are correct," I replied. "In fact, you're wise to consider the consequences of doing what a stranger tells you to do. However, you have to give yourselves up to someone, Social Services or some other government agency. We're licensed private investigators, and I'm also an attorney. If you come with us, I promise to represent your rights as best I can. We'll also try to ascertain the present location of your parents."

"Our mother," Pansy said. "We want to know where Mom is."

"All right," Faye said. "Let's go to the house, where it's comfortable."

I led the way. At first the Isleys walked with Faye, who's the mom type. Halfway along, however, Pansy, trotted up to my side. "Are you really a private detective?"

"I am."

"And a lawyer?"

"Retired."

She was quiet for a few steps. "Is it hard to get through law school?"

I smiled grimly. "Yes."

"So you have to be really smart?"

I turned to look at her. "There are different kinds of smart, but yes, lawyers have to study hard, remember a lot, and learn to be good judges of character."

"Because people lie to you?"

"Yes," I said. "They lie, sometimes in words, sometimes by omission."

"What's that?"

I slowed my steps. "People often know more than they tell. Good lawyers have a sense for the things they don't say." Taking out a tissue, I wiped my nose. Something was pollinating in these woods. I seldom know what causes my sinuses to drip.

"What does the lawyer do if someone lies?"

"It depends on the situation. If the person gets to a point where she trusts the lawyer, she'll probably tell what she knows."

After a pause she asked, "What if she doesn't?"

I shrugged. "It usually comes out some other way, sooner or later."

Glancing at her sideways, I saw Pansy's shoulders droop. The kid was hiding something, and it weighed on her young mind. I put a hand on her shoulder. "In my years as a lawyer I learned that things generally work out if people think hard about what's best for everyone."

"But how do you know what's best?"

I squeezed her shoulder. "It will feel right when the time comes."

CHAPTER FOURTEEN

Faye

The girls seemed relieved to leave the cabin behind, and I guessed they'd been uncomfortable and afraid there. Barb led them through their story while I scoured the kitchen for things I could use to make them a decent meal. Finding ham, eggs, half an onion, and some cheese in the refrigerator, I made a large omelet and cut it into three chunks.

She began by telling the girls the legal system's position on abandoned children. I kept injecting hopeful comments, because Barb's a little scary when she gets going on the law. I knew she was trying to convince the girls they had to tell us more than, "They just left." Still, quoting precedent is no way to make people relax. In my experience, no matter how much they don't want to tell something, kids will tell, given time.

They had almost finished eating when the truck arrived with my horses. Though I was eager to hear what the girls had to say, I went outside to guide my new friends to their new home. They came out of the truck a little skittish, and I couldn't blame them. It was a new place, and I was a new owner. I led the buckskin (I named her Anni-Frid) and the chestnut, (Agnetha, of course—Who doesn't love ABBA?) into two of the four stalls available. Aware of how little I knew about the care and upkeep of horses, I substituted affection for expertise, petting and telling them how pretty they were. It seemed to work.

I returned to the house, where Barb and the girls had washed the dishes and put them away. "They've agreed to come into town with us," Barb told me. "We'll see what Rory can do about finding their parents."

"Our mother," Pansy corrected again. "Ben isn't our dad."

"Okay," Barb said agreeably. "We're going to find your mother."

They seemed encouraged by Barb's positive tone, and we gathered up their things and went outside.

I'd let Buddy out of the car, and he was back at the lawnmower, digging at the dirt around it. "Buddy, come here!" I called. He didn't obey immediately, and I called again. "Bud! We're leaving." Reluctantly he came to the car, where I introduced him to the girls. Iris and Pansy were polite. Daisy was thrilled. "A dog!" she squealed. "I always wanted a dog, but Ben says they chase animals and make them sick."

"Some do," I told her. "You have to teach them not to."

She climbed into the back seat, calling, "C'mon, Buddy! Want to sit on my lap?" Amazingly, Buddy did. He jumped nimbly into the car and onto her lap, giving her an adoring look he usually reserved for me. Iris and Pansy got in on either side of Daisy, patiently enduring her comments about what a great dog Buddy is and how it would be nice if they could have a dog just like him. They agreed, but I could tell they had little hope such a thing could ever come to pass.

"This is a really nice car," Iris said from the back seat.

"Yeah," Pansy agreed. "We don't have to sit sideways like in the truck."

"Did your mom and Ben take the truck?" I asked.

"Iris drove it into the trees," Daisy said proudly. "She didn't even hit one."

I looked at Iris, whose face turned crimson. "We wanted people to think we left," she said, "but I'd never drive on the road without a license."

Rose was gone. Ben was gone. Neither had left in the family vehicle.

Each girl had packed a bag—literally, since they didn't have suitcases. When we got to the house, I put them in our only guest room, which was fine with them, since they seemed to feel better staying together. Using the guest bath, each girl took a shower and put on clean clothes. They looked better, but I couldn't help but notice that their new outfits, though cleaner than before, still screamed rummage sale.

While the girls cleaned up, Barb called Rory to tell him the morning's events. He said he'd call the sheriff's office, since the farm was out of his jurisdiction. He called back to report that Rob Brill, the recently elected sheriff of Milldon County, was busy with a multiple vehicle accident. He suggested Rory talk to the girls about where their parents were.

Rory arrived as I was helping Daisy put her hair into pigtails. She smelled of shampoo and soap, and I hugged her, unable to resist her cuteness. I loved raising boys, but I'll admit it would have been nice to have one little girl to fuss over. "The police chief is going to talk to you," I said, turning her so I could look into her eyes. "You have to tell him everything, okay?"

She nodded emphatically. "It's a sin to tell a lie."

"That's true. Let's go meet the chief."

Rory met the girls in my living room, which we thought was a better choice than an office. He introduced himself, telling the girls he was trying to get permission for them to stay with Barb and me for a few days. I saw Pansy bite her lip at his phrasing. There were no guarantees, but foster homes are always in short supply, and I thought our reputation would serve us well. Once that was established, he set his hands on his knees and leaned forward, ready to listen. "I need you to tell me everything you can about how your parents disappeared."

Iris glanced at Pansy, who gave the slightest of nods. Iris sighed. "A month ago, we came home from school and Momma was gone." She paused, swallowing hard at the memory.

"Where did she go?"

"Ben said she ran away."

Pansy made a small noise of disgust, and her lips formed the word *liar*.

"Pansy?"

She shivered. "Nothing." She turned to Iris, encouraging her to go on.

Iris smoothed her hair, still wet from the shower. "We didn't know what to do. Ben said if anyone found out our mom had left, we'd have to go to Social Services and they'd put us in foster homes. Ben said he'd take care of us if we kept up the work around the place."

"Slave labor!" This time Pansy's voice was audible.

"Pansy." It was less a reprimand than a warning. Their eyes met, and that unspoken communication thing happened again. Biting her lip, Pansy turned her face downward.

Iris went on, still fiddling with her hair. "Ben said school was a waste of time, and the teachers might stick their noses in our business." With a maturity that was heart-breaking for one so young she added, "We tried to keep up on our lessons. We read a little bit every night."

"I can read a whole book!" Daisy announced. "One Fish, Two Fish, Red Fish, Blue Fish."

"That's really good," Rory responded. "You'll have to show me sometime." He turned from littlest to oldest, a question in his eyes.

"We did what Ben said," Iris said, putting a hand on Daisy's shoulder. "I cooked, Pansy took care of the animals, and Daisy helped."

"Did Ben ever—hurt you?"

"No." It was plain Iris knew what he was thinking. "He'd holler sometimes, but he never hit us or—anything."

I heard Barb's sigh of relief. She'd no doubt encountered many abused children in her work as a district attorney, though she seldom spoke of it.

"Ben was never mean," Pansy said, "His friends are weird, though."

"Like who?"

"Nobody hurt us," Iris said firmly, and once again, Pansy closed her lips tightly. "Nobody touched us, nobody messed with us. It was like a deal, you know? We helped out on the farm, and Ben kept us together."

I wondered what was in it for Ben. Was he a good man who'd felt obligated to care for Rose's daughters?

"What happened to your real father?" I asked.

Rory shot me an irritated look, and I recalled I wasn't the interviewer. He waited for Iris to answer, though.

"He died," Iris replied. "Daisy was only one."

Barb picked up on the purpose of my question. "So your mom gets Social Security for the three of you?"

Iris nodded, and Barb gave me a glance of approval. The likely reason McAdams had kept Rose's departure a secret was financial. He wanted the money meant for the girls' welfare.

Rory took the lead again. "Did your mom and Ben ever argue?"

Before Iris could answer Pansy said, "Mom was going to leave him."

"Did she say that?"

"Well, no, but she'd cry sometimes." With a pained expression she added, "We just didn't think she'd leave us too."

Rory sensed it was time to back away from the mother's betrayal. "Okay. We know your mother disappeared last month. When did Ben leave?"

Iris licked her lips, and Pansy spoke again, so abruptly the lie was obvious. "We got up Tuesday morning and he was gone. We didn't know he was leaving and we don't know where he went." Pansy glared into empty space, meeting no one's eyes. Iris examined her hands, clasped in her lap.

There was a brief silence, and Daisy seemed to feel the need to fill it. "He dis-dapeared," she said, raising her hands as if to indicate a magic trick.

"What did he take with him?" Rory asked.

Pansy looked to Iris, who said after a pause that seemed too long, "The suitcase and some of his stuff. His razor, a pair of jeans, and some shirts."

"And his toothbrush," Pansy put in as if that were significant. "He packed his toothbrush."

Rory asked more questions, but that was all the information he got. They got up Tuesday morning and found Ben gone. That was all they could tell us, or all they would tell.

CHAPTER FIFTEEN

Retta

As usual, I was the last to hear what my sisters should have told me right away. I'm always reachable by phone, either directly or by text, and while I can't keep up with my granddaughters in speed, I'm pretty fast and I answer right away. Faye barely knows how to text, and she often turns her phone off because she thinks it saves on the battery. As for Barbara Ann, she refuses to be "on call 24/7" so she ignores her phone when she feels like it. I've given up trying to explain the importance of communication to them.

By the time Faye called, it was almost four o'clock. They'd brought the Isley girls into town and sent for Rory, who got little more from them than Faye and Barb had. After all that, they remembered they have a sister who's been taking care of the old place for years, sends them a check every quarter, and might like to know what's going on out there.

What they should have done was bring the girls to me. In the first place, they knew me, at least a little bit, since I was the person they rented from. In the second place, my home is set up for little girls, since my daughter Alys and her husband Chuck bring Peri and Pola up from Bloomfield Hills at least twice a year. Though Barbara's house is big, it has almost no guest space. She occupies the upstairs and Faye and Dale live downstairs. The Smart Detective Agency (Oh, how I dislike that name!) offices take up a couple of rooms at the front. That leaves only one skimpy room for guests. I suspect that's how Barbara Ann likes it.

Faye insisted the girls were fine with them. "The little one loves Buddy," she told me, "and he's taken to her too."

That was a surprise. Buddy, not the loveliest of dogs by a long shot, has focused totally on Faye since she rescued him from freezing to death on a deserted road. I've tried to be nice to him, as has Styx, but Buddy has the nasty temperament common to strays.

"Don't let her get her face near that dog," I warned. "He might bite her."

Faye laughed out loud. "Right now they're curled up in a chair together eating cheese crackers. I think Buddy knows she needs a friend."

The words friend and Buddy together in a sentence wouldn't have occurred to me, so I changed the subject. "I've been thinking about Rose Isley. I know where the shop she used to have is, and I wonder if the landlord might know if she has family somewhere."

"It can't hurt to ask," Faye said. "I'm going to start supper, but call me if you find out anything." I smiled at the enthusiasm in Faye's voice. She enjoys nothing more than having people to cook for.

I almost pushed the end button, but I heard her say, "Wait! I wanted to let you know Cramer is going to start moving into the bunkhouse tomorrow after work. He wants to get it done over the weekend, so I told him to pick up the key from you tonight."

"I'll drop it off on my way through town," I promised.

"Okay. Dale and I still plan to go out there after supper. I can't let my horses spend their first night in a new place alone."

"You're going to leave Barbara with three little girls?" The image of my old maid sister dealing with that was cause for both humor and alarm.

"She says she'll be fine."

I ended the call, shaking my head. Faye had become a horse owner. Barb was acting as surrogate mother to three kids in crisis. I was heading out to investigate what was certainly a puzzle and possibly a crime. A person never imagines how life can change after fifty.

I remembered Rose Isley's yarn shop because it had shared space with Ellie, a tailor I use for alterations. People think it's great being petite, but just try buying pants that fit or a coat that doesn't drag on the ground. Ellie's great at refitting my garments so I don't look like

I'm wearing my older sisters' clothes. Not that I ever would.

The building, old and saggy, had once been a mom-and-pop grocery store. When that failed, it sat empty for years before finally re-opening as a craft mall. The rooms are divided among crafters from stained glass artists to weavers to stone-cutters, and they take turns minding the store. Some had carved out a niche for themselves, as Ellie had with sewing and alterations. Others, like Rose, had to give up the struggle.

Ellie was putting things away, and checking my phone, I saw it was almost five. "I won't keep you," I promised, "I just want to know who the landlord is for this building."

Looking over her half-glasses, Ellie grinned. "That would be me."

"Really? I didn't know you were in property management."

She shrugged modestly. "A few years back the guy who owned this place got sick and wanted to unload it. After we dickered a little, I got a price I could afford. I figured I'd charge rent instead of paying it, and so far it's worked out okay."

"That's great, first because you're doing well and second because I have questions."

She closed the cash register drawer and removed the key. "I'll try to help."

"Didn't Rose Isley rent from you for a while?"

Ellie nodded. "When I bought the building, she had two rooms on the west side. She did beautiful work, but Rose has no head for business." She ticked off items on her fingers. "In the first place, she practically gave her stuff away. In the second place, she'd get caught up in something she was working on and forget there were orders she was supposed to get done. And in the third place, she often closed up in the middle of the day because of some event at church she felt obligated to help with." Ellie set a box of buttons under the counter. "People appreciate artistry, but they also expect common sense."

"So Rose's business failed."

"We all tried to help her. She had a little income because of her husband's death, but she wasn't much good at managing that either. She'd buy a bunch of stuff from the other artists here and then not have enough for the rent either here or at home."

"Then she met Ben McAdams."

Ellie put things away as we talked. "I suppose he was good for her in some ways because he forced order onto the chaos that was Rose's life."

"They did well together, then?"

She gave a snort of disagreement. "I said in some ways. In others, not so much." A box bumped into place on a shelf below the counter. "I met Ben the day he came to help her move her stuff out. He was nice to look at, but kind of nutty."

"In what way?"

"Well, I saw right away why he lived out in the boonies. He looked like Jeremiah Johnson, and he barely spoke to me. Later, when he thought I couldn't hear, he made a nasty crack about me making money off other people's labor." Ellie held out her arthritic hands. "Do these look like I sit back and rest while others toil around me?"

"So Rose left the co-op and went to live with Ben?"

"Right. She still makes lovely things, but they sell them from home or at craft shows." Ellie grimaced. "They eliminated the evil middle-man: me."

"Did you talk to her after she moved out?"

"Once. We met on the street, and Rose seemed really glad to see me. She said things were fine. Ben was fine. The girls were fine. Her work was fine." With a gesture, Ellie swept away all that fineness. "I think she was miserable, but she didn't know how to change things."

"Too bad," I murmured.

"It's hard to know who to blame," Ellie said. "A man like Ben is domineering, but maybe he gives a woman like Rose the structure she lacks. I worry about those poor girls, though. Just because their mother needs someone to tell her what to do every second doesn't mean they need it too."

CHAPTER SIXTEEN

Barb

As Faye cooked dinner for the girls, she dealt with no less than three hot flashes. Sweater on, sweater off, back door open, back door closed, and so on until the meal was ready. Despite frequent wardrobe changes, she created a delicious meal of home-made chicken tenders, fries, and corn.

The Isleys dug in eagerly, not the least bit shy about filling their plates. My sister has a way of making people feel at home. There's no magic phrase, gesture, or action, but there's never a stranger in Faye's kitchen.

There was hardly room at Faye's refinished oak table for six of us, but we managed. Iris, the perfect lady, sat demurely next to me and made polite conversation. Seated between Iris and Dale, Pansy ate like someone who's been living in the woods should, and Faye made sure she had enough of everything. Daisy sat between Dale and Faye, and Buddy plopped himself next to her chair. From time to time I heard sounds that indicated he was eating, and Daisy's delight with what she thought was a secret was all too obvious. Iris tried to signal her to behave herself, but Daisy was having too much fun to notice. Catching Iris' eye I winked, and she relaxed a little.

Once we finished the meal, the girls began what seemed to be a familiar routine for them, clearing the table and stacking the dishes in the sink. Iris ran hot water in the sink and began washing. Pansy rinsed the dishes and set them on a clean towel. Little Daisy put the ketchup, ranch dressing, and barbecue sauce into the refrigerator and gathered up the placemats, shaking the crumbs into the garbage.

"We have a dishwasher," I protested.

Pansy glanced at the appliance as if it were an alien likely to zap her with a death ray. "Faster this way." I guessed she hadn't used one before.

"I often do dishes that way myself," Faye said. "It's restful, having your hands in warm water, and quiet, too, because everybody leaves you alone for ten minutes."

While the girls worked, Faye brought out the bag she'd packed for a night at the farm. Daisy seemed nervous about her departure, but Faye told her, "I have to leave Buddy here. Can you watch him for me?"

Daisy happily agreed, and Faye showed her where his food and treats are stored, cautioning that he didn't need as many as he thought he did. "We don't want him to get fat," she said, and I rolled my eyes just a little. Faye spoils the dog, and Dale tries to curry his favor by sneaking him treats. Buddy wouldn't get any fatter under the care of a six-year-old than he does with his mom and dad.

Faye signaled me after she said goodbye to the girls, and I followed her onto the back porch. "Don't worry," she told me, though it was obviously she who was worried. "Rory's bringing the sheriff over in the morning."

I smiled at the idea that Rory and the sheriff were my relief squad. "We'll be fine. Take the time you need with your horses."

"Cramer is bringing his stuff out tomorrow after work, so we plan to spend the day clearing the bunkhouse out for him." She frowned. "We might not get back until late. I don't know about supper—"

"Faye, that's what Pizza Hut is for. One phone call and they bring supper right to your door."

She didn't argue, but I guessed she thought I didn't fully understand the nutritional needs of growing children. Dale was already in the car, so she gave me a quick hug and hurried around to the driver's seat. As she got in, he handed her a pair of sunglasses, which she put on. It was after six, and they were heading east. I didn't think she needed them, but apparently Dale did.

Back inside, the girls had cleaned the kitchen and swept the floor. Despite my assurances to Faye, I had a moment of doubt. What time should they go to bed? Was I supposed to suggest activities? Board games? Reading? I had no idea what today's kids do with their evenings.

Pansy solved my problem. "Do you have cable?"

"Um, Faye does. I don't watch much TV."

"We're not allowed to, either." Daisy spoke as if some adult had forbidden television to me. "But when we get to, we like Nickelodeon."

"Well, you're welcome to see if you can find it."

Minutes later, I stood in the doorway to the guest room while Pansy scrolled through the TV offerings with an ease everyone under thirty seems to possess. She found the station, which was playing a show I was vaguely familiar with, *SpongeBob Squarepants*. I stood for a few minutes watching them settle on the bed together. Pansy controlled the remote, Iris took Daisy under her arm, and Buddy jumped up beside her and settled in with a sigh.

"We're good," Pansy assured me. "Do whatever you usually do at night."

Telling myself that kids who'd spent the last three days on their own probably didn't need my direct supervision for an evening of television, I said goodnight and went upstairs.

It was a pleasant evening, and the upper story had heated during the day, so I opened the window in my bedroom to let in cooler air. I was as surprised to see the cat as she was to see me, and we both froze for a second. By the time I realized she was there, she was gone.

Maybe it was having a houseful of abandoned kids, but I felt sorry for the animal. Going to my refrigerator, I found some leftover Tandoori chicken and shredded it into a plastic bowl. In a second bowl I poured water, having read somewhere that adult cats don't need milk. It took some doing to get the screen out of the window, but I figured it out and set the bowls on a spot where the porch roof met the house wall. Pulling the curtain aside I anchored it with a book, turned off the lamp, and waited.

It took a while, but the cat came hesitantly along the roof, sniffing at the wind. When she found the food, she fell on it with a fury, growling to herself as she tore at the meat. The beast was starving.

I had a moment of disgust for neighbors who had let such a pretty little thing go hungry, but the cat probably hadn't approached anyone. Well-camouflaged in shades of brown, black, and gold, she could easily melt into the background simply by lying still.

Once the meat was gone, the cat lapped up the water. I watched, fascinated by the efficient, reverse cupping action of her tongue. We'd had cats as kids, almost a necessity in a house with an abundance of places where mice could get in. Usually there'd been one or two inside cats and many more in the barn to keep the rodent population down. The barn cats were feral, hard to catch and viciously defensive, and I recalled many scratches on my arms from catching them. Remembering how soft their fur felt, I moved my hand toward the stray, hoping to pet her.

The cat was gone in a heartbeat. Leaning on the sill I looked outside, but there was no sign of her. Feeling disgruntled that my attempt to be kind was rejected, I wrestled the screen back into place and retreated to my desk to do some night work.

My current project involved quotation marks, and I reread the letter I'd written.

To the management of Marty's Market:

In recent trips to your store, I have noticed signs that say such things as "FRESH" PINEAPPLES AND *"REAL"* WHIPPED CREAM.

Apparently the idea is to emphasize the words *real* and *fresh*, but emphasis is more properly shown with italics, bold print, or underlining.

Quotation marks surround words that are not the authors' own. In addition to their obvious use around formal quotations like "War is hell," they can be used to show a writer's disagreement with what is said. For example, *I don't agree with what the "experts" say about cholesterol.* Putting the word *experts* inside quotes indicates disagreement with calling them that. The marks also let readers know when a writer is being sarcastic or humorous: *His "remedy" for a cold was a pint of whiskey.*

In either case, the quotation marks mean the writer doesn't want the reader to accept at face value the word or words inside them. Therefore, when you put *fresh* and *real* in quotes, you're telling shoppers either you don't <u>believe</u> or don't <u>mean</u> your pineapples are fresh and your whipped cream is real.

Since this is not the message you intend, I suggest you follow the rules of punctuation.

A Frequent but Disappointed Shopper

At about ten-thirty, I crept downstairs to look in on the girls. Daisy was asleep with one arm over Buddy's back, her cheeks rosy against her pale skin. Iris, too, had drifted off, her head tilted toward Daisy. Pansy looked up as I stopped in the doorway. Pillows propped behind her head, she was watching *CSI*, an old one with Grissom leading the team. From her expression I knew her parents wouldn't approve her viewing choice.

"I used to like that one," I told her softly. "It's gross sometimes, though."

"I'll watch something else," she said, but I noticed she didn't change the channel. "Is being a detective in real life like it is on TV?"

"Not exactly. It's a lot more paperwork and a lot less gunplay."

She chewed at her lip. "Did you ever catch a murderer?"

"Yes." I heard the pride in my voice. "Twice now we've helped put killers in prison."

"Oh. Well, goodnight."

"Goodnight, Pansy." Did I imagine it, or had I seen fear in her eyes when I spoke of catching killers?

CHAPTER SEVENTEEN

Faye

It felt good to wake up in my childhood home. Dale and I slept in what had been my parents' room, and I recalled waking up there as a kid when I was sick. Mom had kept an old cot in the closet, and if she was worried about one of us, we'd be tucked into one corner of their room. Beside the bed would be a TV table with medicine to suit whatever the ailment was, cough syrup, perhaps, or aspirin tablets cut in two. I felt safe in that room, as if the last forty years hadn't happened. Dale hadn't been permanently disabled, Cramer hadn't married an awful woman, and Bill hadn't failed at business so many times he might never recover. Until I opened my eyes I was six again, like sweet little Daisy. Mom and Dad were spooned nearby, ready to protect me from all the ills of the world.

Of course that wasn't true. I rose, shivering in the chilly May morning. Dale slept on peacefully, and I closed the door so as not to disturb him as I went about my chores.

Fighting the feeling I was snooping, I searched Rose
Isley's cupboards and found coffee, sugar, and an ancient,
drip-type pot in four parts. There was a teakettle on the
stove, so I heated water in it as I spooned coffee into the
strainer section of the pot. Setting it into the carafe, I put
the water tank on top, filled it when the teakettle steamed,
added the lid, and waited. Soon the drip, drip, drip that
gives such pots their name sounded, and the aroma of
coffee filled the kitchen.

I took the first cup for myself, stirred in sugar, and
with the mug in one hand, slipped on the canvas shoes I'd
left near the door. I was eager to get out and see my
horses, reassuring them and satisfying myself they were
acclimating to their new quarters.

Closing the door quietly, I headed toward the barn,
sipping at my brew and taking in the glories of a May
morning. Though it was cool, I could tell already the day
would warm. The leaves had really popped over the last
few days, and soon the woods would be opaque, hiding the
activities of hundreds of deer and small animals.

Air smells new in the spring, like life starting up again.
I have to admit, though, that the closer I got to the
barnyard, the nastier the smell got. I wondered how often
the animal pens required cleaning. It would be constant
work to keep them in good shape.

The horses greeted me with soft sounds of welcome.
Anni-Frid came to the gate, nodding as if to say, "Good
morning." Agnetha was a bit less trusting, but when I

leaned on the gate and spoke to her she came over, obviously wondering if I'd brought a treat. I had an apple for each of them, and I set one on my palm, holding it out to her. She took it, munching daintily. I gave Anni-Frid hers, and she did the same. I haven't met that many horses, but I've never met one that doesn't like apples.

When I turned to leave the barn, a man stood silhouetted in the doorway. We both started in surprise, but I recovered quicker than he did, perhaps because I had the moral high ground.

"Who are you?"

He hesitated, and I thought he was deciding how to answer. "Sorry if I scared you," he said smoothly. "I guess you're the new tenant?"

"I'm not a tenant; I'm one of the owners. And you are?"

He stepped inside, and I got a better look at him. "I'm Colt Farrell, a friend of Ben McAdams." I recalled Barb telling me about his visit to the office. "You alone out here, ma'am?"

"My husband's in the house," I said. "He'll be right out." I was remembering a recent situation when a man had trapped me in a barn, intending to kill me.

Farrell didn't seem to have any such thing in mind. "I loaned Ben my chainsaw last month. I didn't think anyone would mind if I took it back."

It seemed logical enough, but something in his manner struck me wrong. Unaware if Dale was even awake

91

much less up, I chose to be non-threatening. "I didn't see a chainsaw here. Maybe it's in the tool shed."

"I'll look there." He turned to go then turned back. "You can come with me if you like, to see I don't take anything else."

"That's not necessary," I said tactfully, "but I'll help you look."

We went through every building, the back porch, and even the root cellar, but we found no chainsaw. Farrell seemed disappointed. "I hope he didn't take it with him. That wouldn't be right."

"No." I looked around the yard. "Where's your car, Mr. Farrell?"

Another pause before he answered. "Over there." A deep blue truck was pulled off the driveway and into the trees, where I hadn't noticed it. "I like to park in the shade. Keeps the interior from fading."

That struck me as unnecessary at 7:30 in the morning, but I merely nodded. "If I find a chainsaw, I'll let you know."

"I'd appreciate that." He backed away, obviously reluctant to give up.

I watched as he went to his truck, got in, and started it up. Farrell waved farewell, and I did my best imitation of a friendly wave in return. As I turned toward the house, Dale came onto the porch. "Who was that?"

"A friend of Ben's, he says," I replied. "But I think he's more snoop than friend."

CHAPTER EIGHTEEN

Barb

Sheriff Rob Brill arrived at my office promptly at ten, with Rory not far behind. The sheriff and I had met a few times, and he seemed a decent man. He also seemed willing to respect me and the agency, which went a long way toward establishing cooperation.

"I spoke with Judge Dean," Brill told Rory and me. "He doesn't see a problem with you keeping the Isley girls here until we find out where their mother is."

"Thank you. This can't be easy for them." Rory and I filled him in on what we knew about Rose Isley's disappearance and Ben McAdams' insistence on hiding it from the world.

Brill pulled at his right earlobe. "I think you're right. Keeping Rose's absence a secret gave him access to her money. But where did she go?"

"That worries me," Rory said. "Do you think she'd leave her girls, Barb?"

"I've never met her, but Retta says she wouldn't, not for this long."

"Mom wouldn't just leave us."

We looked up to see Pansy standing in the doorway. I'd left the girls with my phone, my tablet, and my laptop, hoping they wouldn't notice what was going on in the office until we were ready to speak with them. Pansy must have guessed their future was being discussed. She looked so young and yet so old, and my heart went out to her. I was beginning to believe her mother was dead, and I feared Ben McAdams was responsible.

Rising, I went to her. "Come in, Pansy."

She sat in the chair I pulled up for her, next to Rory and across from Sheriff Brill. After introducing them, I sat back and let Brill take charge. He told her the judge's decision then turned to me. "Ms. Evans, can I ask you to step out of the room for a few minutes?"

"Of course," I answered.

Rory rose with me. "I'll go along and say hello to the other girls."

We left together, aware Sheriff Brill intended to ask Pansy if she was comfortable staying with us. No doubt he'd ask the other two as well, privately so they could voice any concerns they had about the situation.

I led the way to the guest room, knocked on the door, and asked, "Are you decent? You have company."

A voice called out for us to come in. We found Iris lying on her stomach on the bed, typing on my iPad with one finger. I'd introduced her to Amazon Prime, and she was delighted with all the choices.

Daisy sat on a looped rug beside the bed playing with Buddy, and he seemed like a puppy in her presence. As he ran circles around her, making huffy noises and displaying silliness quite unlike his usual grumpy behavior, I was reminded he wasn't very old. They say every kid needs a dog. It might be just as true that every dog needs a kid.

"Where's Pansy?" Iris asked.

"The sheriff had to speak with her alone for a few minutes."

Iris' response startled me. "No! She can't!" Springing up from the bed, she pushed past Rory and ran down the hallway. He followed while I went to Daisy, whose mouth opened wide, warning tears were imminent.

"It's okay, Sweetie," I told her. "Everything is okay."

It didn't work. Starting with a low moan of grief, Daisy's voice rose to a full-blown wail. Though I have little experience with children, I know there are times when only a reassuring hug will help. I took Daisy into my arms, and she leaned into my shoulder, sobbing. As we sat there together, rocking gently, understandable words emerged. "Don't put Pansy in jail! She didn't want Ben to get dead."

CHAPTER NINETEEN

Retta

Knowing Faye intended to spend the day cleaning and clearing the bunkhouse for Cramer, I decided to go out and help. Dale tries to be useful, but he usually just follows Faye around and gets in her way. When I show up, he generally finds somewhere else to be. With him out from underfoot, Faye and I would get the place spiffed up in no time.

I took Styx along, figuring he could spend the day digging holes to his heart's content. At home I fill in his excavations, but on the farm it doesn't matter. It's so cute to see him go at it with both feet and come up with dirt all over his big old face. Of course it's not so much fun when he rides home in the car all dirty, but it's worth it to see him happy.

We arrived around nine-thirty, and Faye told me about her uninvited visitor. "That's just rude!" I said. "He should ask before snooping around, even if he is retrieving his own property."

"Barb checked him out." Faye was already poking around in the bunkhouse, deciding what Cramer might be able to use. "He owns an electronics store in the strip mall on 10th, and he's an elder at the church Ben and Rose attended."

"That's not a ringing endorsement." I shivered. "Churches with made-up names make me nervous."

Faye paused to look at me, one brow raised. "The name of every church was made-up at some point, Retta, even ours."

I let that one go. "Okay, he was looking for his chainsaw. I guess we accept that unless we can prove otherwise. Now let's get to work."

We spent hours moving, sorting, and cleaning. Originally a dormitory, the bunkhouse had become a storage place when the need for extra beds disappeared. Things that should have been thrown away or donated were taken out there to rot or seize up from temperature and humidity changes. Faye and I made two piles on the grass, one for trash and one for the Salvation Army. Luckily, one thing we found in the bunkhouse was a dolly, so between us we managed to get even big items like ancient cook-stoves, broken dryers, and battered chests of drawers outside.

Dale tackled the bathroom, which was more like a locker room than a bath. There were three toilet stalls and three sinks on one end, and a shower tree at the other. He worked to get the shower, one sink, and one of the toilets fixed and scrubbed clean.

Faye thought Cramer might want the large, ornate table that had been our mother's pride and joy. The top needed refinishing, but the result would be much nicer than the junk they sell at big box stores. There were only three chairs left of the set, but she said that was plenty for a man who needed to think a while before taking up with another woman.

We were hauling a box of odds and ends outside when I noticed Styx sniffing at the lawnmower again, pawing at the dirt around it. "He sure likes that thing."

Faye paused to wipe her forehead with her sleeve. "Buddy went over there, too. Something must be—" She paused as realization hit. "—buried there."

Images spilled into my mind: Ben McAdams and Rose Isley quarreling. Ben striking out. Rose falling. Had she hit her head on something? Had he beaten her to death in a fit of rage? I feared we were about to find out.

"Not something. Someone!" I whispered.

Faye went toward the barnyard gate, where a shovel sat propped against a fencepost. "See if you can move that mower."

The rider wasn't much different from my own, just a lot older and rustier. I found the shifter, put it into neutral, and rolled the thing off to one side. The patch of ground Styx was so interested in was strewn with hay, which was odd now that I thought about it. Parking an old mower on a pile of hay is practically inviting a fire when you start it up again.

Using the shovel, Faye scraped the hay aside. The ground had been disturbed fairly recently. Marks showed where the dirt had been patted into place. "Oh, Lord!" Her face stiff with dread, Faye began digging.

Going to my car, I got a pair of gloves I keep there and returned. Taking the shovel away from Faye I told her, "My turn." She backed away, panting a little from exertion.

About a foot down, the shovel struck something, and my stomach did a flip-flop. It wasn't hard, like rock, but it definitely wasn't soil. It was something that didn't belong there.

Kneeling, I dug with my gloved hands until a scrap of color appeared in the brown dirt. It was an afghan, hand-made in blues and greens. As I gently scraped the dirt away, the outline beneath it appeared. A nose, a chin, a forehead. A person.

Somehow it seemed more respectful to peel the blanket back from the side, taking the final layer of dirt with it. Faye knelt beside me, grasping the cover near the bottom, and we pulled it away together. First a pair of jeans appeared, then a plaid shirt.

The face we revealed wasn't Rose Isley's, as I'd expected. It was Ben McAdams.

CHAPTER TWENTY

Barb's call came moments after Retta and I made our grisly discovery. "Faye," she said, speaking softly so she wasn't overheard on her end, "the girls did something to Ben. We're not sure what yet, but we're pretty sure he's dead."

When I told her what Styx had led us to, Rory got on the phone and ordered us to wait for the sheriff to arrive. I could have told him I knew that much about crime scene investigation, but I merely agreed.

They were there in twenty minutes, first the sheriff, then an ambulance (much too late), and finally Rory in a city police car. Barb had stayed with the girls, and I imagined her irritation at being relegated to baby-sitter. Rory had called a child psychologist the department used in such instances and asked her to go to the house. None of us knew for sure yet what those three innocent-looking children had done, but they'd need counselling, no matter what.

The EMT spoke to Sheriff Brill in quiet tones. "Okay," Brill replied. "Do what you have to do to get him out of there."

Brill came over to where Rory, Dale, Retta, and I stood. "Broken neck, it looks like. There'll be an autopsy, but the guys think it's what killed him."

"It can't be the girls' fault," I said, aware of my desperate need to believe they'd done no wrong. "They couldn't break a grown man's neck."

"We'll look into it." Brill's tone was non-committal. "Doc says there's a suitcase under the body. Somebody tried to make it look like McAdams left the area." He glanced at the spot where Ben lay. "Those girls need official supervision."

Retta went into what I call her act, though I have no doubt she'd argue with the terminology. When Baby Sister wants something from a man, things happen. Her hair seems to get shinier, her eyes start to glow. The way she stands becomes provocative, though I swear she makes no discernable movement. All I know is suddenly Retta isn't a widow of almost fifty with two grown children. She's a sexy, sweet young thing, and most men turn downright goofy. I've never understood how she does it.

"Sheriff, wouldn't it be easier on everyone if the girls stay with us? Faye and I raised children, so we understand their needs. Barbara is a retired district attorney, a registered private investigator, and she has served as a

Milldon County deputy." She turned to Rory. "Isn't that right, Chief?"

Rory is somehow immune to Retta's charms, and I detected a glint of humor in his eyes. "Ms. Evans is very competent."

Brill tried to remain professional, but judging from his expression, Retta would get what she wanted if he had anything to say about it. "I need to talk to the judge, but I think he'll listen to me."

Retta gave him what she'd call a grateful smile. Some might call it a simper. Whatever the term, it usually works.

When we got back to the house, Barb brought the two older girls into the office, leaving Daisy with Buddy and Dale in the kitchen. It was good that Buddy liked Daisy, because he wouldn't have been pleased to see Styx making himself at home in his domain.

There was some shuffling as we arranged chairs for eight people and space for a very large, very determined dog. Finally we were settled, Styx resting his head on Retta's knee. Barb had several fresh tissues in hand, possibly for her postnasal drip, but more likely preparation for removing dog drool from her office furnishings. The only reason Styx was allowed was that his presence made the girls less nervous.

Brill nodded at the psychologist, Julie Walters, who said gently, "Girls, we need you to tell us everything that happened, starting with the day your mom—left."

Pansy's jaw set, but Iris said, "You found him, didn't you?"

"Yes," Brill said. "His neck is broken."

"We didn't do it!" The words came from between Pansy's teeth.

"Just tell us what happened," Julie said softly. "You're not in trouble as long as you tell the truth."

Pansy started to say something, but Iris spoke first. "We need to tell, Pansy." Shifting her slight shoulders, she began, "We already told you we came home from school and Momma was gone."

"Mr. Yates lets us off on the road," Pansy put in. "He doesn't like turning around in our yard, and we don't mind walking. We came up the drive, and there was Ben, pacing back and forth like a grumpy, ornery old bear."

Once again Iris cut off Pansy's negative description of McAdams, probably fearing we'd suspect she killed him. "When he saw us coming he shouted, 'Your mother's run off!'"

"We didn't believe him at first," Pansy said, "but he took us in the house and showed us. Her things were gone, her favorite necklace, her nightgown, and some of her clothes."

"How did he explain her absence?"

"He said they had a fight. I knew Momma wasn't happy by how quiet she was lately." Iris heaved a sigh as if we'd gotten to the hard part. "Ben said we had to keep it a secret or we'd get split up." Her eyes reddened, and Julie moved on.

"So you kept quiet."

"We thought if we waited, she'd come back—"

"She didn't just leave us!" Pansy insisted. "He made her do it!"

Something passed across Iris' face, and I guessed she feared it was worse than that. My throat closed as I thought of the things she'd kept to herself for her sisters' sakes.

"You didn't know what to do," Julie prompted.

"He said she might come back." Iris brushed her hair away from her brow. "He said he'd take care of us, even though we aren't his. We could stay on the farm."

"And wait for your mother to come home," Julie said, and Iris nodded. How she must have prayed that would happen!

Pansy spoke again. "Ben said we couldn't go to school because they might figure things out from something we said. He said school's a waste of time, especially for girls. Animals teach us everything we need to know to get along."

Rory's curiosity was piqued. "What did he mean by that?"

"Well, animals don't have a government. They take care of things without committees or counselors or cops. They fight it out when they need to, and the strongest wins. And the males dominate, because that's the way God made them."

"I see," Rory said. "Do you agree with all that?"

"Not me," Pansy said. "Ben's full of beans, and his friends too."

Rory smiled at her blunt honesty, and Julie moved on with the interview. "So you stayed and helped out on the farm."

"Yes." Iris glanced at Pansy then back to the psychologist, and I saw in her eyes things she couldn't admit. "We didn't like it with Ben, but at least we were together."

"I bet Mom wrote to us." Pansy's eyes were hard. "I bet he tore up the letters. That's why he just had to get the mail himself."

McAdams had isolated the girls. Somehow he'd accessed Rose's finances so he could spend their money any way he pleased.

"Okay," Julie said. "Let's talk about what happened to Ben." Both girls looked down at their hands. "You need to tell us."

There was a long silence. Looking down at her hands, Pansy finally said in a small voice, "Ben died because I ran away."

"Why, Pansy?"

She shrugged as a tear fell onto her lap. "Ben had some friends over to play cards. He sent us up to bed, but later I had to use the bathroom, so I came downstairs. I was going to just slip by, but Ben was talking about our mother. He said he hoped she never came back, because he was better off without her."

Sensing there was more to be told, Julie simply waited. Iris looked as if she might say something but instead put a knuckle to her mouth and stared at the items on my desk.

Pansy's voice went flat as she continued, "One of the men, Sharky, said to Ben, 'You ever want to get rid of a girl, I'll take the middle one. I could use some help around the place.' His voice sounded funny, and it scared me real bad."

We avoided each other's eyes, shocked by the revelation.

The story spilled out then, as if Pansy could no longer stop it. "I waited for Ben to say I'd stay with my sisters, but he didn't. Instead he laughed and said, 'Yeah, Pansy's a good little worker.'" She looked up at us, her eyes bright with tears. "I thought, *What if Ben lets him take me? What if that man comes upstairs tonight and makes me go home with him?*"

Julie swallowed once before asking, "What did you do, Pansy?"

She'd recovered a little, and she clenched her fists. "I went out the back door. It was cold and I was barefoot, but I didn't care. I was going to go to the cabin and wait until Sharky left, but then I thought, if I wasn't there when he went to get me, would he take Iris or Daisy instead?" A flash of anger lit her eyes. "I should have gone back to bed, and then if he came up there, I'd have kicked him where it hurts and told him to do his own dumb chores!"

Julie's gaze remained steady. "Where did you go?"

Her lip quivered. "I climbed up the silo." Faye gasped, since poisonous fumes can build up in a silo, but Pansy reassured her. "If it's empty, you won't die. I climb up there sometimes when Ben's in town so I can look at things. It's like being a bird." She scrubbed one hand across her eyes, wiping away tears she refused to acknowledge. "I thought I'd watch until they left and when Ben fell asleep, I'd get Iris and Daisy and we'd run away."

I pictured Pansy, cold and scared, perched precariously thirty feet in the air, fearful her sister would take her place as that awful man's "girl." If Ben McAdams hadn't already been dead, I might have had a go at him myself.

"It took a long time, but they finally left. They were pretty drunk. One of them said something about Ben learning to drive a boat. We don't have a boat, but like I said, they were drunk."

I wanted to ask if she could be more specific, but I didn't want to distract her.

"I thought Ben would go to bed," Pansy went on, "but for some reason he looked in our rooms and saw I wasn't there."

"He woke me up," Iris said. "He asked where Pansy was, and I said I didn't know. He told me to go back to sleep, but I couldn't."

Pansy took up the story again. "Ben came outside and started hollering, 'Pansy! Pansy, where'd you go?'" There was an air of dread in the room as we all realized what was coming. Pansy's voice cut in and out, but she kept on. "He had this big old light, and he started shining it everywhere. I stayed real still, but my nightgown is white, and he looked up and saw me sitting there."

"He told you to come down."

She nodded. "At first he just said I should. Then he ordered me to get my—to get down. He was so mad I got even more scared. I just kept shaking my head."

"So he started up after you."

"I heard Ben shouting and came downstairs," Iris said. "When I went out on the porch, he was climbing the silo. He had the light in one hand, and he was shouting at Pansy, saying what he was going to do when he caught her. I screamed, 'Leave her alone!'" She was crying, but she got it out. "His foot slipped, and he—"

"He fell," Pansy finished. "He hung on for a while, but then he—"

We all imagined the horrifying sight of watching Ben lose his grip and drop to the ground. "It was my fault," Pansy finished. "If I hadn't gone up there, he'd be okay."

"No, it's my fault," Iris insisted. "I scared him. That made him fall."

Rory cleared his throat, and I sensed he wanted to assure the girls neither of them was at fault and everything was going to be fine. There was, however, the question of why they hadn't called for help. "When you got to Ben, he was dead."

"Yes." Iris's voice was a whisper, but she recovered somewhat and finished the telling. "We'd started digging a bed for rhubarb at the front of the house, so we dug it down some more and put him in there. We put some of his things in there too, so if anyone came looking for him it would seem like he packed up and left."

"Does Daisy know?" I asked.

"We told her about it when we got to the cabin. We had to, because she was scared he'd be mad and come after us."

"What made you go out there?" Rory asked.

"I wanted to keep running the farm," Pansy said. "If we could do it without Mom, I said we could do without Ben, too. But Iris thought people would figure out we were on our own."

Iris' hands fluttered, unconsciously recalling their indecision. "We talked about it all night. Then Pansy thought of the cabin, and I typed a letter to Mrs. Stilson, saying we'd all moved away."

I recalled Retta mentioning Ben's crude writing skills. Now that I thought about what she'd read to me, the wording sounded like the work of children. Thank you for being a nice landlady.

"You thought it would keep people from looking for you."

"We were just going to stay until Mom's June check came in."

"When we figured out a way to get the money out of the bank, we were going to take a bus somewhere," Iris added.

"Florida," Pansy said decisively. "It's warm down there all the time, so you don't have heating bills."

"But you couldn't leave the animals on their own," I said.

"No," Pansy seemed irritated with herself. "Iris didn't want me to, but I sneaked back and fed them. Daisy wanted to come the last time, and that's how you saw us. She isn't as fast as me."

I gave Barb a sharp glance in case she intended to correct the poor kid's grammar at this tragic point in time. She was silent.

Iris turned to Sheriff Brill. "What's going to happen to us now?"

"You're too young to live on your own," Julie said gently.

The sisters looked at each other. "If we can stay, I know we can keep the farm going." Pansy turned to Retta. "We'll pay the rent every month, honest!"

"It's not a question of the money, Pansy. You need someone to care for you."

"We don't need anybody!" Her voice rose, and Iris put a hand on her arm again. "Well, we don't!" Her tough persona failed, and she dissolved into tears.

Brill nodded at Julie, and she rose from her chair. "Let's go to the kitchen and see if Mrs. Burner has any sodas."

When they were gone, Retta said, "Sheriff, you can't be considering charges."

Brill pulled at his earlobe, signaling an attempt to make a decision. "Well, they failed to report a death, but they are just children."

"Children who've suffered mental abuse at the very least," Barb said. "They shouldn't be forced to endure separation as well."

Retta seemed pleased that she and Barb were on the same side for once. "Why don't I take the girls home with me? It will take a few days to sort this out. Barbara and Faye can look for Rose, and I'll see if the girls know something that will help us locate her."

"Or her body." Barb spoke the words I'd been thinking. "My guess is McAdams killed her, possibly by accident."

No one disagreed. Brill said, "I'll get some search dogs out there first thing tomorrow."

"Poor Rose!" Retta was the only one in the room who'd known the living, breathing Rose Isley.

Brill licked his lips. "I think the judge will be inclined to accept your proposal, Mrs. Stilson. Custody will be temporary, of course, but I agree it's best for the girls right now to stay together, preferably with someone they know and trust."

"Someone at their church might take them in," Barb said. Retta shot her a look, but Barb felt we might give the girls false expectations if we kept them with us. She's said before that investigators can't go around offering shelter to victims, no matter how much they'd like to. It isn't professional.

"What if that pervert Sharky is a member of the congregation?"

That ended the argument. The last thing we wanted was for the girls to be handed over to some weirdo who believed females were put on earth only to serve men.

"I'll make some calls," Brill said, "for now they can stay with you."

Retta had them ready to go in no time. Daisy was sad to leave Buddy but happy to go with Styx. I just hoped the big dog didn't squash Daisy in his eagerness to welcome her to his home.

Iris made a polite speech of thanks to Barb, Dale, and me. She looked pale, as if the stress of the past few weeks was taking a toll on her. Pansy seemed determined to avoid emotion, but I hugged her anyway. After a few seconds she returned the embrace, clasping my waist tightly.

Barb told Pansy, "You girls did nothing wrong. The law and anyone with a jot of common sense knows that accidents happen."

Barb can use words like *jot* and get away with it.

Pansy didn't reply. Between my hug and Barb's assurances, I hoped we'd eased the child's mind.

Watching them pile into the SUV, I decided a trip to Retta's might be exactly what the girls needed. I doubted the Isleys knew what it was to be girly, but they were about to find out. The next time we saw them, I fully expected bright fingernails, complicated hairdos, and clothing not previously worn by someone else. The Isley girls were about to learn the art of conspicuous consumption.

.

CHAPTER TWENTY-ONE

Retta

We spent a quiet afternoon at my house, getting used to each other. The girls were shy at first, but Styx was a big help. Daisy laughed out loud every time he did his paws-on-shoulders routine, despite the fact she generally stumbled backward under his weight until she bumped into a wall. Pansy and Iris loved Styx too, so he was in his glory with lots of pats and pets.

The girls could have had their own bedrooms, but they chose to sleep in the king-sized bed in the lavender one. Once we'd set their bags in there, I took them to the den and left them alone for a while, figuring they needed some down time. Pansy turned on the TV—something I'd never seen in their house on the farm—and they settled in on the couch.

While they unwound, I went outside to do some chores. I'd bought sets for my flower boxes a few days earlier, and I thought it was safe to plant some of the pinks along the south-facing wall.

I'd been at work for perhaps twenty minutes when Iris came outside. "Want some help?"

I almost said, "Go enjoy being a kid," but I guessed she needed something to do. So far in her short life, Iris had been expected to stay busy. Now she probably felt at loose ends.

"Great," I said. "There's another trowel beside the garage door."

We worked together for a while in companionable silence. The sun was warm on our backs, and the dirt yielded easily to the tools. I had already set the plants in place for the arrangement I wanted, so it was simply a matter of digging a hole, adding a little fertilizer, setting them in, and firming the soil around them.

When we finished Iris said, "I'll get water if you have a bucket."

"We'll use the hose," I replied, guessing she was used to lugging buckets of water. "There's a spigot around the corner."

I hauled the hose out of storage and hooked it up. Iris uncoiled it then watered the plant plugs so they'd settle into their new home without harmful air pockets around their roots. We stood back to admire our work, and Iris reached down and gently brushed some mud from a tiny leaf. "You like growing things," I said.

She nodded. "You put a seed or a plant in the ground. It makes itself at home and gives you something back: food, ground cover, or flowers." She rubbed her dirty fingers on the back of her skirt. "I'd rather work in the garden than talk on the phone." After a pause she added, "Or do math."

Though I agreed, it's a bad idea to tell kids it's okay to hate math. "Which classes do you like?"

"English," she replied immediately. "I love stories about monsters—Dracula, Frankenstein, Pogrebins."

I didn't get the last one, and I guessed Ben McAdams wouldn't have approved of her reading choices. Taking up a rake I'd set out earlier I said, "The other beds haven't warmed up enough for planting yet, but I'm going to get them ready."

"I'll help." She took a second leaf rake from its place on the garage wall, and we headed to the back of the house. As we worked I asked, "What was Ben like?"

She shrugged. "He was okay, I guess. Not like a dad, though."

"You remember your own dad?"

She bit her lip. "Pretty well. Pansy kind of does, but she says it's just little bits. Daisy was a baby when he died, so she doesn't remember him at all."

"He was killed in a car accident?"

"Yeah. We were on our own for a while, and money was really tight. Mom met Ben at church, and he seemed real nice. He'd buy us dinner after service—just McDonalds, but still. After a couple of months, he took us all out to the farm." Her gaze drifted as she remembered.

"It was June, and it was so pretty out there, you know? The trees and all the flowers."

Our mother prided herself on her flowerbeds, and I recalled the profusion of blooms she left behind: peonies and daffodils, tulips and hyacinth, snowballs and lilacs. I could almost smell them myself, and I had a moment of nostalgia for the place. Maybe I wasn't the same girl who'd hated living on the farm. Maybe my own flower beds were proof it had influenced me.

"Pansy went crazy for the animals," Iris was saying. "Back then Ben just had chickens and cows, but she was out there getting to know them ten seconds after we arrived."

"Ben asked you all to move out there with him."

"He said what a great family we made, and how we could live the way the Lord intended, growing food and taking care of the land."

"She agreed to live with him but refused to marry him?"

Iris sighed. "She said if we ever had to leave, she didn't want him to have any hold on us."

"How did he take that?"

"He was really grumpy. Pastor Cronk kept taking Mom into his office for private talks. Afterwards she'd tell me what he said."

"And what was that?"

She frowned a little as she tried to get it right. "Pastor said God wants the church to bless the relationship

between a man and a woman, but Mom said God is
patient, so He wouldn't mind if she thought about it for a
while."

"It sounds like your mom didn't quite trust Ben." Iris
didn't answer, and I asked, "Was she right about that?"

"Like I said, he was never mean, but he was kind of
weird."

I spoke casually. "Weird how?"

"A lot of the time he didn't talk. Sometimes we'd go all
day without Ben saying anything except yes and no. Other
times he'd talk for hours—at least that's what it seemed
like. It was almost like a sermon, but sometimes it didn't
even make sense."

"What kind of things did he say?"

Iris stooped and picked up a stone that had found its
way into the flower bed. "He talked about being a good
Christian a lot, but Ben drank beer—a lot of it. Sometimes
he got into fights at the bar, and once he came home with a
big old black eye. He didn't talk to any of us for about two
days." She pulled tangled vines from the rake's teeth. "He
lied sometimes, too."

"Lied?"

"Yes. Like at first, we thought he owned the farm."

"He told you that?"

"Nobody remembers him saying it, but—"

"He let you believe it."

"Right." She attacked a corner, angling the rake to
remove a clump of wet, rotten leaves. "He talked like the

farm equipment belonged to him, but later we found out it didn't."

"No. It belongs to Mr. Masters."

Iris smiled. "He's nice. In the winter he makes sure we have enough feed for the animals."

"Did Ben ever hurt your mom?"

"No. He always said women are weak and need a man to protect them." Iris paused, leaning on the rake handle. "All the men at church say stuff like that."

"About women being weak?"

"They say how precious we are and how God wants them to cherish us." Her brow puckered. "But my teacher says men who only let women do what they say are bullies."

"You girls were only supposed to do what Ben wanted."

"Mom, too." Her eyes narrowed as she sought an example. "We had a car at first, but Ben said Mom had to sell it. He took the money and bought this old truck. Said it was more practical."

"For the farm."

"Yes. He had Mom put the truck in her name, but she wasn't supposed to drive it because women aren't very good drivers." She paused, remembering. "Ben drove, Daisy sat on Mom's lap, and Pansy and I had to sit on the little sideways seats in the back."

"Not very comfortable for five people."

"It was just a pain doing everything his way, you know? Lately we did most of the work on the farm, but Ben still gave the orders."

"Was he busy with something else?"

She shrugged. "I guess."

"I know your mom paid the rent. Did she handle the money?"

"Yes, but she had to show Ben what she spent at the end of the month." Bitterly she added, "And it was mostly our money!"

While Iris went to get the wheelbarrow we'd left at the front of the house, I thought about how a man like Ben McAdams keeps a woman under his thumb: fear of being alone, fear of financial insecurity, fear of making him angry. Often those fears make a woman afraid to leave, afraid even to speak up.

When she returned Iris said something that revealed she hadn't been as willing as her mother to trade freedom for a place to live. "I wrote about the things Ben said once for English class, and the teacher kept me after. She said if he ever got mean I should let her know, but he didn't. He told us what we had to do, and we had to listen to a bunch of stuff about the wrong kind of women."

"What did he mean by that?"

She rolled her eyes. "It's really weird."

I smiled at her. "I can deal with weird."

Her answering smile was brief. "Well, women are ruining the government, Ben said. Ever since they got the vote, things have gone bad. Men can't find jobs because women take them. Women vote for stupid programs like Social Security and welfare and laws about global warming, which Ben doesn't—didn't believe is real."

"But didn't Social Security support you after your father died?"

"Yes."

"And Ben thought it was okay to accept that money?"

"He said if the government's dumb enough to give money away, we should take it. But he says—I mean, he said—him taking us in was proof that if the government didn't stick its nose in, people like my mom would figure out how to survive."

"Living with a man she didn't love and being his slave?"

Iris gave me a funny look, and I realized I'd said too much. While I'm nowhere near Barb's level of feminism, I was still irritated by Ben McAdams' view of women.

"I guess we all see things differently," I said in a lame attempt to be fair. Taking a new grip on my rake I said, "We'll finish this bed then go inside for a cold drink."

CHAPTER TWENTY-TWO

I was alone in the office Saturday morning. For weeks Barb had planned to drive to Flint to visit an old friend. She'd considered cancelling, but I insisted nothing would happen over the weekend that required her presence. It's sad when you have to encourage another person to relax and have fun once in a while.

The phone rang around nine, and I answered with my usual, "Smart Detective Agency, Faye speaking."

There was a pause then a voice said, "Mrs. Burner? It's Gabe." Gabe has to get up his courage just to speak to me, since he's convinced I dislike him. While he's half right, he's also half wrong. Gabe is growing on me—slowly, I admit. At first I thought he was evil. Then I decided he was merely annoying. Now that he's our part-time employee, I'm working my way to Gabe being only mildly irritating. However, once a guy kidnaps a person, she's likely to have trouble warming up to him.

"Hello, Gabe," I said. "What can I do for you?"

"Well, I went out to the farm, like Mrs. Stilson asked me to, but there's people out there. I thought you should know."

"I'm so sorry, Gabe. I guess nobody remembered to let you know my son has moved in out there. He'll take care of the animals."

"Oh."

"We'll pay you for going out today, since it's our mistake."

"Thanks. It was just kinda funny, you know? Mindy and me went out there, and we saw those three men coming out of the barnyard. I didn't know whether to shoo 'em off your property or not, but they jumped in a green truck and left before we even got out of her car. I didn't know it was your son."

I glanced at the clock. Cramer is a night owl, a late riser on weekends, and a very sound sleeper. "That wasn't my son, Gabe. You say there were three men?"

"Yeah. One was pretty big, one was skinny like me, and the driver was kind of medium-size with dark, curly hair."

Colt Farrell.

"Thanks for the call, Gabe. I'll get a check out to you."

"Um, could I come and pick it up this afternoon? I got a truck payment due."

"Sure. I'll have it ready, but come to the back door. We close the office at noon on Saturdays."

My first instinct was to call Barb, but I stopped myself, knowing she'd turn around and come back. Instead I called Rory at home. By rights I should have contacted the sheriff, but when you know a police officer personally, and he knows you don't create drama just to stir up excitement in your life, you gravitate toward him, even if the case isn't in his jurisdiction.

"Good morning, Faye," Rory said. "Did Barb get away all right?"

"She did." I told him about Farrell's second visit to the farm.

"Well," he said, "technically it's trespassing, but I doubt you called me to propose a slap on the wrist for Mr. Farrell."

"I just wonder what kind of person he is." Cops usually know who should be arrested as well as who has been. I wouldn't strain our friendship by asking outright if Farrell was a criminal type who had yet to be caught, but I hoped Rory got the hint.

He chuckled. "I bought some speakers from his store once. It's called Mr. A.I., like artificial intelligence, but most of his stuff is pretty run-of-the-mill. All I can tell you about Farrell is the speakers he sold me worked."

CHAPTER TWENTY-THREE

Barb

As I drove southward, in and out of spits of rain, my thoughts remained in Allport. I was worried about what would happen to the Isley girls, I was curious about where Rose was, and I was irritated with my sister Retta.

My plan had been to have a pleasant weekend. I'd meet an old friend, attend a show at Whiting Auditorium with her, and recall old times.

Then Retta had called, and what should have been a carefree trip became care-laden. Baby Sister's view of my weekend was quite different from mine.

"I understand you're off to Flint tomorrow," she'd begun. When I affirmed that, she said, "Don's mother has a birthday on Wednesday, and I thought you could drop off my gift to her. It will be a lot more personal than the mail or UPS."

"Retta, your mother-in-law doesn't know me from Mary Poppins."

"Sure she would, once you tell her who you are. You two have met at least three times."

"Over twenty-eight years. That doesn't make us friends."

"No, but she'd love to see you. She's really lonely, and it would be so nice for her to have someone stop by. You could stay and visit for a while. You'll just love her."

"Isn't she active in her church?"

"Oh, yes."

"And didn't you say she plays dominoes with a bunch of women?"

"Twice a week."

"She doesn't sound lonely to me."

"Well, no, but she doesn't get to see family very often."

"I'm not family."

"You're almost. She told me once how much she admires you."

"When was that—in 1998, at your Christmas dinner?"

"Maybe." She sounded pouty. "It's only twenty miles out of your way, Barbara. You could make an old lady happy with just a few hours of your time."

"No."

"Barbara—"

"Retta, I'm not visiting your mother-in-law. If you want her birthday present personally delivered, get in your car and drive down there yourself."

"I've got the girls now," she said stiffly. "I just thought since you were passing so close, you wouldn't mind helping me out."

"Well, I do mind."

That was the end of the conversation, but it had pretty much wrecked my mood. It was clear Retta considered me a selfish brat willing to ignore a nonagenarian's birthday. How anti-social is that?

CHAPTER TWENTY-FOUR

As I was locking the front door at noon, I heard Gabe's voice at the back. When I entered the kitchen, Gabe was standing just inside the door, his shirt damp from rain. Dale had just invited him to stay for lunch. It wasn't the first time this had happened, and I wondered again what my husband saw in the Smart Detective Agency's slightly goofy go-fer.

Dale dished up a third bowl of the chili I'd made the day before and set it before Gabe. Handing him the envelope containing the money, I took my own place at the table. Dale set eight crackers next to my bowl before passing the rest of the packet to Gabe.

"Chili smells great, Mrs. Burner."

Gabe and Dale began discussing the problem he'd been having with his truck. I put the crackers to one side; I don't care for them with chili, but Dale does.

"I put a new carburetor on," Gabe said, "but it don't sound right."

"How's the mix?" Dale asked.

I stopped listening then, so uninterested in Gabe's gas mix I could hardly stand it. I'd finished lunch by the time my companions remembered I was there. While Dale got him a second bowl of chili, Gabe asked, "Miz Evans out on a date with the chief?"

Imagining Barb's dismay at Gabe's casual mention of her social life I replied. "No. She's visiting a friend."

"Oh." In typical Gabe fashion, his mind went off on its own track. He shoveled chili in for a few seconds then asked, "Did you ever think about the chief being a chief?"

"What?"

He spoke slowly, as if I had a comprehension defect. "He's the chief of police, and he's an Indian too, so he might be—" He waved a hand, palm up, "—another kind of chief."

Dale apparently thought that was the funniest thing he'd heard all week, and they snorted like teenagers. I just looked at them.

Gabe finished his bowlful and stood. "I'd better go. Mindy has to shop for a new outfit for some conference she's going to, and I'm supposed to give advice."

"A conference?"

"Something for work." Gabe and Mindy met while he was in jail. Mindy was a student then but had since become certified in social work. While I had yet to meet her, I had some opinions about her future in social work.

Dale walked Gabe to the door, slapping him on the back and reaching forward to open it for him. "Come again, son. It's good to talk to you."

Watching Dale's half-smile as Gabe headed to his truck, I realized what my husband liked about him. Until his accident, Dale's days had been spent with manly men who advised each other on fixing their cars and lived in a world of machines and machismo.

Dale now lived with two women in a place of soft voices and dim lights. In the first few months after his injury, his friends had come to visit, but in time their lives had gone on in the old way, the way Dale could no longer participate in.

Gabe wasn't exactly an old chum, but he was male and he loved talking cars. I resolved to make him more welcome next time, not as an employee, but as Dale's friend.

CHAPTER TWENTY-FIVE

Retta

Saturday morning was cloudy with rain off and on, so I decided the Isleys needed a little retail therapy. I drove them to the mall, announcing that everybody got one completely new outfit. Iris expressed doubts about accepting gifts, but I told her, "I love shopping for girls. You have to let me do this."

Allport's mall isn't much, but it has a couple of stores that appeal to the young set. Iris chose a longish denim skirt, a plain white top, and lace-up shoes. I'd have to work on her fashion sense.

Seeing Pansy petting some glittery jeans on a table, I asked, "Do you like those?"

She removed her hand. "We're not allowed to wear pants."

"If you like the jeans, get them," I said. "We can always exchange them if you decide you'd rather have something else."

Shifting through the pile, she chose a pair with rhinestones on the back pockets. "Are these okay?"

I chuckled. "They are if you think they are."

It was probably wicked of me to undermine their parents' rules, but I had a feeling it was Ben who'd made them up, and Ben was dead. If their mother was still living, she might accept that a pair of jeans wouldn't result in her middle daughter's ruin. And if Rose was dead, as Barbara Ann was pretty sure she was, the girls' world was going to change drastically. A pair of jeans wouldn't matter.

Daisy was fun to buy for. She was excited by all the choices offered, and she looked darling in everything. In the end we bought yellow leggings with a matching yellow-and-navy overdress with ruffles around the bottom.

"Can I wear my new stuff now?" she asked.

"Certainly. It's fun to get new clothes, isn't it?"

She nodded. "Momma makes us things, but I only get them when they're too small for Pansy."

Having been the littlest sister, I know how boring it is to wear your siblings' hand-me-downs. I'd had my share of new clothes as a kid, but I'd also had my share of Barb and Faye's castoffs. It's a pain to not get to choose your own style.

Along with buying for the girls, I picked up some items that would look stunning in Barbara Ann's office. I even went with her taste, which is okay though a little outdated. I chose two hurricane lamps in Victorian blues and lavenders and a set of vases with genteel ladies and gentlemen in silhouette around the bases. I added some pillows for the window casings, to soften the perpendicular lines.

Knowing she'd see the improvement if the items were in place when she walked in Monday morning, I planned to slip in and add the items myself. While I wished I could be there when she saw how much more comfortable the room looked, I wanted it to be a surprise.

Laden with our purchases, we made our way to the small food court. I let each girl choose a shop and buy her own lunch. After much discussion, Iris and Pansy went off to get pizza. Daisy stayed with me, and we visited the A&W for foot-longs and fries.

Once we'd eaten the main meal, I suggested dessert. Iris went for a frozen yogurt while Pansy got a root beer float. Daisy and I chose cones with sprinkles. Returning to our tables we licked, spooned, and slurped in relaxed ease. Watching them, I thought how resilient children are. Though they looked like any kids might on a shopping trip, they'd been through a lot. They had more trials to face, and I was pleased to provide them an island of comfort between their scary past and their sad future.

"If we were home right now, we'd be working in the garden," Pansy said, stirring her drink with her straw. Iris jerked slightly as if reminding herself not to enjoy the moment too much.

"Do you like living on the farm, Pansy?"

"I like animals." Frowning, she asked, "You're sure they're okay?"

"My sister's sons are out there. They'll see to them."

"And the garden?" Iris asked. "It needs a lot of attention or the weeds will choke out the little plants."

"They'll see to that, too," I told her, hoping Cramer, Bill, and Carla knew carrots from pigweed. I doubted they did, but it was no longer Iris' job to worry about it.

"Are they living in our house?" Daisy asked.

I was honest. "Someone has to be there to see to everything."

She nodded, her eyes downcast. It had to be hard knowing someone new was in what the girls thought of as home.

"We tried to take care of things after Mom left, but we were getting low on feed." Pansy glanced at Iris. "We told Ben about it, but he didn't act like he cared."

Daisy wasn't keeping up with her ice cream, and I foresaw disaster for the new outfit. Noticing, Iris took the cone from Daisy's hand and licked around the outside to remove the melted part. When she handed it back, Daisy took a lick and said, "Ben was busy, 'cause he was fixing up the cabin for us."

"It's not like we asked him to." Pansy's tone was resentful.

"It was nice of him, though," Iris said, her tone so mom-like I smiled. "He made us a playhouse, and we should be grateful."

"Ben was remodeling the cabin for you?" Going out of his way for the girls seemed out of character.

"He kept buying stuff and hauling it down there, but it was a big secret," Pansy said. "We weren't allowed down there, but when he finally let us see it, it didn't look that different."

Iris was still trying to be grateful. "He fixed the door, and he built bunk beds."

Pansy shrugged. "It didn't seem like it was worth the time he spent down there. A new door, windows, and bunks. That's all."

"There's another door inside the bed." Daisy was doing better at keeping up with the drips.

I looked at Iris, who seemed surprised. "What door is that, Daisy?"

"You can't see it unless you move the mattress," She gave her cone another lick. "It's a trapper door, like in *Aladdin*."

CHAPTER TWENTY-SIX

Retta called just after lunch. Dale had gone back to his workshop, and I was baking cookies. Relaying the girls' story and Daisy's mention of a "trapper door," she strongly suggested I investigate. Setting the whole sheet of cookies in the fridge, I headed back to the farm. I figured Daisy had probably misinterpreted some hardware in the bunk and concluded it was a door, but I didn't mind satisfying Retta's curiosity. I'd meant to go out there that afternoon anyway, to check on my horses and see Bill and Carla, who'd arrived from Chicago in the early morning hours.

I parked in the driveway next to Bill's ancient CRV, which was packed to the roof with boxes and tubs. Attached was a rental trailer containing what looked like the rest of their belongings.

Cramer came out of the barn, carrying an empty bucket. "Hey!" he called out. The knee-high rubber boots he wore were a wise choice for a barnyard in spring. Over a gate post hung a flannel shirt he'd shed, since the afternoon sun had become quite warm.

"How are you coping with the menagerie?"

He shrugged. "Almost everybody's been fed—not that it will keep the peacocks from complaining."

As if on cue, we heard a cry that sounded a lot like "Help!" The male came strutting out from behind the shed, very much the master of all he surveyed, at least in his little pea-brain. Next came the hens, a few steps behind, like repressed wives.

The house was silent. "Are Bill and Carla up?"

"Haven't seen them. It was almost dawn when they got in."

"I'll look in on the horses first," I said.

Nodding, Cramer went on to the shed with his bucket. Side-stepping barnyard hazards, I made my way to the barn and, squinting into its cool exterior, approached the horse stalls. "Want to explore a little?" I asked.

Snapping a lead rope onto the halter, I led first one then the other to the paddock attached to the barn. Anni-Frid did a little dance of joy when she stepped out into the sun. Agnetha followed more sedately, but she shook her head as I released her, looking around at the new surroundings.

I spent a few minutes with them, letting them get used to me in this new setting and wondering if I might possibly ride after thirty years out of the saddle. I didn't want my horses to forget their training, but I couldn't help but notice how high their backs were off the ground. A fall at my age wouldn't be pretty. Might the Isley girls come out and exercise them? That would give them a chance to see their former home again, and I wouldn't have to risk my neck—or a hip.

"Hey, Mom!" I turned to see Bill coming out of the house, dressed in rumpled sweats. Meeting him halfway, I embraced him. Like Cramer, Bill is tall, but he carries less weight. He'd grown a beard, and I gave it a playful tug. "New look?"

"I was going for farmer, but Carla says I look more like a deranged lumberjack." He gestured at the car and trailer. "After we talked about it, we decided we didn't need the expense of two trips. We brought everything on this one."

"Things went okay?" It was my way of asking if they'd gotten out of their lease without legal difficulties.

"No big problems. We'll see a lawyer to make sure everything's ironed out." He yawned behind a fist. "Sorry. Not much sleep."

"I saw your phone message when you got in."

"I kind of heard you pull in, I think." Having finished his chores, Cramer approached to give his brother a manly hug that lasted all of one second. "I'll help you unload your stuff later."

"We'll have to move the previous tenants' stuff out first." Turning to me he asked, "Did these people just abandon the place?"

"At least one of them is dead." I gave a brief recap of the situation, ending with, "The littlest girl claims there's a trapdoor in the cabin. I'm going down there to see if she's correct."

"Do you want us to come along?"

I gestured at the loaded vehicle behind me. "Looks like you have lots to do right here."

Carla came out of the house, wearing jeans and a Northwestern sweatshirt and pulling her long, black hair back into a low ponytail. I noted gray streaks, though she was only thirty. Carla would never consider covering the gray, and on that we agree. Barb and Retta can do as they like; I earned every one of my gray hairs, and the world is welcomed to look at them.

After hugging me and Cramer Carla offered, "I can make coffee. There's a really cool tin pot in the kitchen, and I want to try it."

"I'm on a mission," I said, "but when I get back, I'll see how well you manage it."

"It's a long walk, if I remember," Bill said.

"Not as long for an adult as it was for a kid. You guys go ahead and get your stuff unloaded. I won't be long."

Leaving them to the task, I headed up the hill, rounded the barn, and took the path to the cabin. This time there were no girlish voices, and I entered alone, flashing the light I'd brought with me around the interior. Going directly to the bunk-beds, I knelt and pulled the foam pad off the bottom one. "She's right," I muttered. In one corner there was a hasp, padlocked to the bed frame.

I glared at the lock, stymied. If the trapdoor was Ben's secret, he'd have kept the key with him, probably on the ring the sheriff had found in his jeans pocket.

Glancing around the room, I looked for something shiny. Many people hide a spare key in case they forget or lose the first one. I'd done that a few times myself over the years.

I searched the cabin, feeling along the rafters and examining the walls. After encountering a lot of dirt and many cobwebs, I spotted it almost at the ceiling. Hung on a finish nail, the key blended with the tone of the wood. It was unlikely anyone would notice it, and I could just barely touch it if I flattened my body against the wall and reached up as far as possible.

After a few tries I managed to slide the key off the nail, but it dropped to the floor. I spent a few more minutes lighting the floor with the flashlight in order to see where it fell. I found it in a corner, moved to the trapdoor, and knelt again, unlocking the padlock and removing it.

I felt a moment's dread at the thought of what I might find down there, but I decided if there was a dead body I'd have smelled it by now. The trapdoor was heavy, and I couldn't lift it from my crouched position. Standing, I braced my legs, gave a mighty heave on the handle, and pulled upward. When the door was perpendicular to the floor, I gave it a nudge with my hip, sending it onto the bed frame with a crash. As the sound echoed through the cabin, I knelt again, eager to see what was below.

It was a bunker. A crude wooden ladder led down to a dirt floor perhaps eight feet below. The light from the plastic windows didn't illuminate the space, but I directed my flashlight into the hole. Perhaps ten by ten, the space was half-filled with boxes and crates stacked against the wall opposite the ladder.

With what I'd learned over the last few days about McAdams, I should have known he'd be prepared for Armageddon, whatever that meant to him. It might be terrorists, but it might just as easily be zombies, aliens, or the "gov'mint."

Climbing clumsily down the ladder, I explored the contents of the bunker. There was food, of course, and bottled water, stacked on a rough shelf supported by stakes driven into the earthen wall. One corner contained a chemical toilet, with the appropriate supplies stacked beside it. An army cot lay folded along one wall, and beside it were a couple of rifles wrapped in clear plastic, presumably to keep them in working condition. Two plastic tubs in another corner held a rolled sleeping bag and camouflage clothing: pants, a jacket, gloves, a hood, and a pair of boots. There was no provision for a woman or children. It was a bunker for one.

The tubs sat on a wooden box about four feet by two feet, and I set them aside to examine the box. It had three latches. Two were the loop-over-a-catch kind common to briefcases. The center one required a key, but the key was taped to the end of the box. I removed the tape, unstuck the key, and used it to open the latch.

Inside was what looked like an over-sized shotgun. Near its barrel, four nasty-looking projectiles rested in packing foam cut precisely to fit their outlines.

A soft rustle behind me served as warning, and something shifted in the beam of my flashlight. I meant to turn, but before I could, a terrible blow landed just above my ear. I fell to the dirt floor, unable to move, think, or even protect my face from the impact. Pencil-thin strips of light came and went. Noises seemed to come from far away. I was pushed roughly aside, and I felt rather than heard my groan of protest. Feet stepped around me. Metal snapped against metal; wood scraped against wood. More steps, and the ladder groaned as weight shifted on and off its rungs. My brain was only beginning to recover when I heard, "If you're a good detective, you'll find a way out of there."

The trapdoor slammed shut, and a metallic snap indicated the padlock had been set back in place. Steps sounded on the wooden floor above. Then there was nothing.

CHAPTER TWENTY-SEVEN

Barb

Though I had anticipated seeing my friend Shirley for some time, I was distracted as I drove south. What if Rose Isley was still alive somewhere? Was I wasting time reliving the past when I should be working to find her?

At my age I miss very few rest areas, and each time I stopped, I checked for phone messages. There was nothing from Faye all morning, which meant everything was fine.

Shirley was preparing lunch when I arrived, so I sat in her kitchen as she worked. We spent a while catching up as we sipped iced tea. It was good to laugh at our young selves and the things we'd done, said, and believed.

It was just after one when my phone rang. Shirley was clearing away the dishes, and I excused myself to answer. The caller ID said it was Retta, but it was Pansy's voice I heard when I answered. "Ms. Evans? I have something to tell you, and Mrs. Stilson is busy. She said we could use her phone if we needed to."

"Okay." I was pleased she'd chosen to tell me something first, before she told Retta. Iris was sweet and

Daisy was cute, but Pansy was a sharp little cookie, and it appeared she trusted me.

"What is it, Pansy?"

"We're at your house. Mrs. Stilson is inside and Mrs. Burner is gone, but I think I saw Sharky drive by."

My first thought was Why is Retta at the house? Chiding myself for being overly suspicious, I focused on what Pansy had said. "Are you sure it was Sharky?"

"Well, no. Iris and Daisy didn't see him at all, and I just got a quick glimpse. This guy drove by in an old beater, and he was stretching his neck to look like Sharky does, you know? Like a turkey buzzard pecking at road kill."

On one hand, I trusted Pansy. On the other, I couldn't think of a reason Sharky would drive by my house. It was possible her fears had turned an innocent passer-by into the monster she feared. With all that had happened to her lately, it was understandable.

"It might have been Sharky," I said, "but it might not. You shouldn't worry about it."

"But what if he's looking for me—for us?"

"I can handle him," I said, "and I'll be back home tomorrow afternoon. If you see him again, though, tell Retta to contact Chief Neuencamp. It's very important that we locate him."

"I will," she vowed. "I want to be a detective, like you."

That made me smile. "Thanks for the call, Pansy."

Shirley drove into the city, showing me the sights. Though I enjoyed her company, I couldn't stop thinking about what was going on at home. Had Pansy really seen Sharky? Might he have plans to kidnap her? Should I warn Retta to be extra vigilant?

I hate it when people constantly check their phones for messages. It seems to indicate they're looking for someone or something more interesting than the person they're with. Still, I sneaked a look at my messages several times that afternoon, once while Shirley visited the restroom and twice while she was trying on clothes. Nothing.

CHAPTER TWENTY-EIGHT

Faye

"Mom?" Cramer's voice was the sweetest thing I'd ever heard. "Mom, are you in here?"

I'd promised myself my sons would come looking for me, but when it finally happened, I sobbed aloud with relief. Rising stiffly from the corner where I'd sat for almost an hour, I used a two-liter water bottle to bang on the trapdoor. "Under the floor! Take the mattress off the bottom bunk!"

Cramer found the trapdoor easily enough, but he called out, "There's no key."

They'd tossed it. The hopeful feelings I'd begun to let grow were squashed back into the pit of my despair. I heard Cramer pulling at the door, grunting with the effort. "There's no place to get a hold," he said. "And there's nothing to use for a lever."

I thought about the rifles I'd seen earlier. Could I load one, shoot through the trapdoor, and destroy the padlock? I doubted my marksmanship, having last fired a gun several decades ago, and there was also the fact that I had no idea how to load a rifle.

Cramer was thinking more logically. "I saw some bolt cutters in the tool shed," he shouted. "I'll get them." Pausing, he asked, "Will you be okay?"

"Yes," I called. "But hurry."

I've always had a fear of heights. I hate bridges and skyscrapers and roller coasters. This new experience was revealing another panic-inducing fear. For those first few minutes after the trapdoor slammed, I'd thought I might lose it completely. It was hard to breathe, though I could see the ventilation holes Ben had dug in the walls and feel the fresh air they provided. Knowing they were there wasn't enough. My chest still felt like it would explode. My arms and legs twitched with repressed fear. I tried to dig my way out for a while, but with only forks and spoons for tools, I'd been unable to even make a start on the hard-packed walls.

The tiny logical part of my mind that remained whispered that Cramer or Bill would come looking when I didn't return. I struggled to remember what I'd told them. Had I mentioned the trapdoor? Had I told them the trapdoor was hidden by the bed frame? I couldn't recall, but they'd figure it out. At least that's what I tried to believe.

I held onto my sanity by singing. Recalling lyrics and thinking up the next song kept my mind busy, allowing me to avoid turning into a raving lunatic. Mostly I sang hymns, but I threw in some Blondie and a little Doctor Hook for diversity. It took everything I had not to give in to panic, but belting out "The Cover of the Rolling Stone" helped a little.

The last stretch of time was easier, knowing Cramer would return. I followed him in my imagination: Out the door, through the woods, down the road that circled the barn, and into the tool shed. Once he found the bolt cutters, he'd stop and tell Bill the situation, and he and Carla would return with him. I imagined them coming up the slope, around the barn, through the woods, and back to the cabin. I tried not to hurry them, but it felt like eons before there were steps above me again.

"We're here, Mom." Cramer was panting from exertion. "I had trouble getting to the bolt cutters because we moved so much stuff out to the shed." Metallic sounds accompanied his words, and I heard the snap that signaled the end of the padlock's usefulness. With rattles and thumps, the lock disengaged from the hook, and I heard it clunk as Cramer tossed it onto the plank floor.

I rose from my corner, knowing I should stay out of the way but unable to do it. I wanted out of there more than I'd wanted anything for a long time. When the heavy door rose and light spilled down on me, I started singing Sting's, "If You Love Somebody." Always willing to support me in my craziness, Cramer sang backup as I climbed the ladder.

Our song didn't keep me from bursting into tears as I hugged my sons and blessed the daylight.

CHAPTER TWENTY-NINE

Retta

When Cramer's name came up on my phone, I assumed he had a question about the farm. "What's up, dude?"

"Aunt Retta, I thought I'd tell you what happened before you hear it somewhere else." He explained about Faye's experience at the cabin. "I'm taking her to Sheriff Brill's office as soon as the doctor finishes looking her over." In that helpless tone men get when they have to deal with a crying woman he added, "Carla's with her."

"You're sure she's all right?"

"Yeah. She was plenty scared, though."

"Who wouldn't be? Thanks for the call, Honey."

I pressed end, grateful there was at least one person in my family who found it important to keep me up to date on things like the attempted murder of my sister.

Iris, Pansy, and Daisy were outside, playing with a paddle-ball set I'd dug out of the garage. Iris and Daisy took turns with one paddle, since there were only two, while Pansy waited impatiently for them to find the ball and send it back her way.

"Girls, we need to go into town," I called. "I'm pretty sure Sheriff Brill is going to need to talk with you again."

CHAPTER THIRTY

Faye

My sons insisted I go to the walk-in clinic and be checked out for possible concussion. Once I was pronounced fit, Cramer drove me to the sheriff's office. He'd called ahead, so Sheriff Brill and Rory were both there. The four of us sat in a small conference room trying to put together bits and pieces that, so far, made little sense. They sipped coffee or soda, but for some reason I couldn't get enough water. Cramer noticed, and as I got close to the bottom of a bottle he'd rise quietly, go down the hall to the machine, and get me another.

We went over what I knew, which wasn't much. The attacker had been male, and he'd probably hit me from above, because I hadn't heard him on the ladder. He'd used some sort of club, perhaps a tree branch, since I had a small cut that the doctor said wasn't something a fist would cause. There might have been more than one guy, but only one spoke. He or they hadn't intended to kill me but hadn't worried about whether I died in that awful hole either. The weapon I'd been looking at was now missing.

"That's likely the reason someone followed you out there," Brill said, pulling at that earlobe. "McAdams built himself a secret bunker and hid it down there. Somebody wanted it bad."

"Why?" I was confused about both Ben's reason for having such a weapon and someone else's willingness to kill me to get it.

"We've got a few of that type around here—guys prepared to survive if things fall apart."

"When things fall apart," Rory corrected. "Guys like McAdams are convinced they will." He turned to me. "Describe the weapon, and be as specific as you can."

I tried, but I lacked the proper terminology. I said things like "really big bullets" and "kind of like a shotgun." Rory and Brill glanced at each other.

"Sounds like an M-79," Rory said. "Legal if he'd registered it, but grenades definitely aren't intended for the general public."

Brill reached for the phone. "Nearest place to get one of those would be Grayling." Into the receiver he said, "Lila, can you connect me with someone over at the National Guard base? Tell them I need to know if they're missing any munitions."

While Brill waited for the call to go through, Rory explained what I'd seen. "An M-79 is a grenade launcher that's small enough to conceal. It packs a pretty good punch, a 40 millimeter shell—a grenade—that can travel up to 400 yards." He cupped his chin in one hand. "How many shells were there?"

I scrunched my face, trying to picture the case. "Four, I think."

Rory sighed. "Somebody could do a lot of damage with four of those things."

"It would be helpful to know what McAdams planned to aim them at," Brill agreed. His call went through, and he spoke into the phone. "Sheriff Brill over in Millden County. I have a citizen here that discovered an M-79 hidden in a shack on her property." He paused to listen. "Four rounds, she thinks."... "That's just it, Colonel. Before she could call us someone knocked her on the head and took it." He changed the phone to his left ear and took up a pen with his right hand. "Sounds like you're missing one."

When Brill hung up, his face was grim. "As a good-will gesture to our allies, we offer our facilities for training. They had some foreign troops in last month, a group from Latvia, and after they left, there was a discrepancy in the number of M-79s the colonel thought he had and the number he actually had."

"One launcher missing," Rory guessed.

"Right. They looked into it, but the colonel figured one of the generals helped himself to a souvenir. Nobody wanted to make a big deal out of it. You don't accuse your allies of theft."

Rory shifted in his chair. "You think the visiting troops provided an opportunity for someone from here to cover his theft."

"The colonel is sending us a list of people who were on duty at Grayling during the session."

"Sheriff?"

We turned to see Retta in the doorway. Behind her were the Isley girls, decked out in new clothing. The two older girls had shorter hair than they'd had yesterday. Iris had a blunt cut that framed her face and highlighted her eyes. Pansy had pink streaks in a short, spiky style that made me dread Barb's reaction.

"It's a good thing Cramer called me." Retta's tone hinted she was used to being left out.

"I would have," I defended myself. "I didn't think the girls—"

"They're here because they're the best source of information the sheriff's got." She gestured briskly. "Come in, ladies."

Brill seemed okay being bossed if Retta was doing the bossing. He turned to Rory. "Should I see if I can get Julie down here?"

Rory gave me the briefest glance of bemusement. "Can't hurt."

The room was getting crowded, so I told Cramer he should go. Giving me an extended hug, he said in my ear, "That was scary. Let's not do it again."

"Fine with me!" It was hard to let go of him, but I told myself I'd been a big girl for too long to turn into a shrinking violet now.

As we waited for the psychologist, Rory and I took drink orders for the newcomers. By the time we'd dug up enough change for the machines and returned with sodas, Julie was on her way. At Retta's insistence, I repeated the account of my ordeal, letting on that I hadn't been in the bunker long before Cramer found me. I also left out the grenade launcher entirely. I'd tell her about that when the girls weren't around. The older girls looked embarrassed at hearing about Ben's secrets. Daisy lost interest early on and began counting the ceiling tiles softly to herself.

"You poor thing," Retta clucked over and over, stroking my arm. It's embarrassing to be treated like a child at fifty, but she's like that. When I finished she patted at my hair, which was no doubt a mess. Retta would have come out of a similar ordeal looking like Angelina Jolie in Lara Croft, Tomb Raider.

Julie arrived, looking younger than before in jeans and a tank top, and settled into the chair Cramer had vacated. Sheriff Brill questioned Iris and Pansy about the renovations Ben had made on the cabin. They reported they hadn't been allowed near the place from early spring until a week or so before Ben disappeared.

"He acted like it was more his place than ours," Pansy told us. "He said we should keep it nice and not go moving stuff around."

"Did any of Ben's friends help with the cabin?" Brill asked.

They looked at each other. "I don't think so," Pansy answered.

"That's why they've been searching the property," I said. "They knew he had—" With the girls in mind I changed my wording. "—things hidden, but they didn't know where."

"What's the big secret?" Pansy demanded. "Is Ben a bank robber or something?"

A brief silence followed her question, but Rory stepped in. "We think he was planning a crime, Pansy, and there might have been others in on it. Can you tell us who Ben hung around with?"

"Well, Sharky's the one—the one we don't like much. Mr. Farrell came over a lot, but he pretty much ignored us unless it was to say, 'Girl, bring me another beer.'" A natural mimic, she captured Farrell's arrogance and misogyny in those few words.

"Who else?"

Pansy frowned. "Floyd. I don't know his last name. Do you, Iris?"

"No. He's big, though."

"Real big," Pansy affirmed. "Ben wasn't small, but he looked it next to Floyd."

Iris seemed unhappy with their inability to give us specifics. "You could ask Pastor. He might know."

It was a good idea—as long as Pastor Cronk wasn't in on whatever they planned to do with the grenade launcher. Glancing at me, Retta said, "We'll see if he can help us."

"Was Ben a good shot?" Brill asked.

"Really good," Pansy said. "When he was in the army he got all kinds of medals for shooting."

"Did he belong to the National Guard?"

She shook her head. "He said the military is bad because now they let women in. He had to spend all his time protecting girls who couldn't pull their own weight."

"But they taught him to shoot," Iris added. "He liked that."

If there was mischief afoot, Ben was the likely marksman. That's why he had the grenade launcher, though he probably wasn't the one who'd stolen it.

Brill was checking his computer. "Here's the list the Guard sent over. No one named Colt Farrell on it." He squinted at the list again. "And no one named Floyd. The other one is Sharky?"

Iris said, "I think it's a nickname. He kinda looks like a shark."

Brill leaned toward the screen. "So we don't know Sharky's real name and we don't know Floyd's last name."

Daisy paused her counting. "His name is Floyd Stone, but Mr. Farrell calls him Grave Stone. I asked Ben why, and he said because Mr. Stone is as quiet as the grave."

We fell silent at the thought that Ben was headed for his own grave. It lasted only until Daisy hit the bottom of her drink and made a loud slurping noise. The group laugh she got was more tension relief than anything else.

Brill finished his perusal. "No Stone on the list, either."

"Sharky has to be the thief." Rory turned to the girls. "What can you tell us about him?"

"He's creepy," Pansy said. "You have to walk way around him, because he'll grab you and tickle you, even if you ask him not to."

"Did Ben like Sharky?" Rory's voice was deceptively casual.

After some thought Pansy said, "I don't think so. Sometimes it seemed like he wanted to tell Sharky to leave us alone, but he'd put his lips together and keep quiet."

"And your mother?"

"When they came over she'd send us upstairs as soon as we got our chores done. Lots of times Mom slept with Daisy, because they'd get real drunk."

Another silence followed as the adults in the room struggled to accept the things some children learn to live with. Finally, Brill set rather delicate hands on the desk before him. "Mrs. Stilson, I think we're finished with these young ladies for now. Thank you for bringing them down. Girls, you've been a lot of help."

Retta wasn't about to be dismissed just when things were getting interesting. She cast about the room, clearly looking for a way to stay. "Ms. Walters, I'd like a few minutes with the sheriff before I take the girls back home."

Julie smiled graciously. "Let's go outside, girls."

Once they left she asked, "What's next, Sheriff?"

"We try to find out what those guys were up to."

"No reason to believe their plans are in the past," Rory said. "McAdams' death threw them, but they came after the weapon. I'd say someone else will use it, though maybe not as efficiently as Ben would have. They haven't given up on making trouble."

"So I repeat, what are we going to do about it?"

Rory's brows rose at Retta's inclusion of herself in the investigation. Brill said, "Mrs. Stilson—"

"Retta, please." She gave him that smile again.

"Retta." Slightly flushed, he went on. "We have no evidence anyone's plotting treason or mayhem."

"They stole that grenade thrower thing from the National Guard."

"That's a guess."

"They attacked Faye and left her in the bunker to die!"

"She didn't see who hit her. My people are processing the scene, but unless we find something to connect the attack to one of the men the girls named—" He left the statement hanging.

Retta didn't give up. "We caught Farrell trespassing. Twice."

"And he claims he was looking for property Ben borrowed. Poor grounds for arresting a law-abiding local businessman."

160

Retta made a disgusted noise. I was frustrated too, but he was right. I rose from my chair. "I should get home. Dale will worry."

"Are you sure you're all right, Faye?" Retta hovered at my elbow as if I might collapse at any second.

"I'm fine. Rory's going to give me a ride home. I'll call you later."

It was no surprise when she said, "We'll follow you over there. Daisy can visit your dog, and we can figure out what to do next." I couldn't help picturing Retta tucking me into bed with a water bottle at my feet.

CHAPTER THIRTY-ONE

Barb

Shirley and I arrived at Whiting Auditorium to find the place filling with theater lovers. The show was good, as Whiting's productions always are. I'd have enjoyed it more if I hadn't kept wondering what was going on at home.

After the show we went her back to Shirley's house, where we chatted for an hour before heading to bed. The guest room was comfortable, the house was quiet, but my sleep wasn't restful. In the first place, I'm not at ease in someone else's home, no matter how much I like them. In the second place, my mind kept returning to Allport, to the case that wasn't really a case.

Neither of my sisters had texted or called all day. While I told myself they were simply giving me free time, it felt odd to be out of touch with them. If Faye found any trace of Rose Isley, she'd let me know. If Retta got a bit of information from the girls we could use to find their mother, she'd text. Rose's disappearance had become a personal crusade for all of us. Slapping one of Shirley's pillows into a different shape, I asked myself yet again,

What happened to the mother of those three lovely little girls?

CHAPTER THIRTY-TWO

As Rory drove me home, he made a recommendation. "You and Dale should get away from Allport for a while. I find a change of scenery helps me clear away bad images, so they don't replay like film on a loop."

I thought about the bad things he must have seen in his years as a Chicago cop, which helped me put my experience into perspective. I'd survived. I wasn't hurt. With time, I'd be okay.

Rory was skeptical when I suggested Barb didn't need to know about my adventure while she was miles away. "I'll tell her the whole story when she can see for herself that I'm okay."

"I've never lied to her." He frowned at the car ahead of him. "It's probably not an easy thing to do."

"It isn't," I agreed. "If she calls and asks what's going on, make like Eliza Doolittle and stick to your health and the weather."

Retta's car was parked outside my house, and I groaned. No doubt Dale had already heard the story from her, which made things ten times worse. With a grimace of understanding, Rory escorted me inside. Retta met us at the door, fussing about what a terrible time I'd had, patting my arm, and making me nervous despite her attempts to be caring.

One look at Dale told me he was a basket case, and Rory and I both set about trying to calm him. Despite our best efforts Dale blamed himself, saying he should have gone to the farm with me. I couldn't see how he'd have prevented what happened, but logic doesn't apply when someone we love is threatened.

As I searched for a way to reassure him other than repeating I was fine and it was over, I decided Rory was right: leaving town might be good for both of us. If new vistas could dull the terror I experienced each time I thought about how I might have ended up in that bunker, I was all for it.

When Rory, Retta, and the girls finally left, Dale was still upset. After he repeated for the fifth time that I might have died in that place, I asked, "Do you want me to quit the agency, Hon?"

Dale doesn't move his head much since it disorients him, but he made a negative motion with his hand. "Barb would go on alone, which would drive you crazy." He managed a weak grin. "Besides, I think you like sticking your nose in other people's business."

"Only when they ask us to!" I was relieved that he saw how important the agency was to me, but I knew he'd also counted the times my life had been in danger because of it.

"How about if you and I take a mini-vacation?"

Dale frowned. "You'd leave the middle of all this?"

"In the middle of what? There's no case for the agency, and the police are investigating the little we know. What can we do?" I ran a hand through my hair, wincing when I inadvertently touched the lump behind my ear. "Tomorrow's Sunday. Barb won't get home till late, and Retta mentioned she's taking the girls to church. You and I could take a drive and get a little R&R."

He liked the idea. "Maybe we could go up the lakeshore and stay somewhere overnight."

"We could," I said. "After we visit Harriet, of course."

Dale grinned again. "Of course."

Though I don't like to text, I sent Barb a message rather than calling or leaving voicemail. Despite my flippant advice to Rory, I don't lie well to anyone, and I cannot lie to Barb. Even on the phone, I'd feel like her direct gaze was seeking out my fibs and omissions, and the whole story would spill out. My text was simple: DALE & I ARE TAKING A LITTLE VACATION. WILL SEE YOU MON PM.

I spelled all the words correctly. Barb has no tolerance for texting shortcuts, though she admits a revamping of English spelling is long overdue. She has a little story she tells about Sir Walter Raleigh's plan to oversee such an undertaking. Sadly, he offended the king and got beheaded before he could follow through.

Retta says if Walter was as persnickety about English as Barb is, it's no wonder they chopped his head off. In my opinion, Raleigh could have revamped all he wanted. It wouldn't have made a bit of difference once texting came along.

CHAPTER THIRTY-THREE

Retta

It was late when Faye called, but she's a bit of a night owl, especially when she's got things on her mind.

"Dale and I are going away for an overnight trip."

That never happens, but I got it. "That's probably a really good idea. Any idea where you're going?"

"North, I guess. Dale likes the area around Mackinac."

"Do you want me to call Barbara and—"

"No!" Faye cut me off. "Barb is not to know any of what happened until she's back home."

"She'll be mad," I warned.

"She can be mad. Do not tell her. In fact, don't even call her."

"Well, one of us has to. She'll suspect something if she doesn't hear from us all weekend." I paused to think. "I'll tell her you lost your phone and—"

"Retta," Faye interrupted. "I texted her already, so do not call her and do not text. If you do, I'll tell her that when Rory first came you told him she liked him, just like it was junior high."

"I was very discreet about it," I said, stung. "Barbara Ann would have done her Ice Lady act until Rory wandered off after some other woman."

"That might be, but she wouldn't like knowing you interfered."

"Encouraged," I amended.

"Okay, encouraged. Just don't talk to her again until after I do."

Who knew Faye could be so bossy? I knew she meant every word, though. "Okay, but I'm going to pretend I lost my phone, because she's sure to call and ask me where you are."

Faye chuckled. "She'll never believe you went five minutes without a phone, but go ahead. Give it a shot."

Stung by her attitude I said, "You know, Faye, you could just ask. You don't have to threaten to tell on me."

"I know. It's so junior high, but a girl's gotta do what a girl's gotta do."

CHAPTER THIRTY-FOUR

Barb

Shirley had arranged a surprise that made me cringe on the inside, though I pretended to be delighted. She'd invited two women we'd gone to college with for Sunday brunch. That meant I wouldn't be able to get away until noon at the earliest.

Not only was I anxious to get home, I wasn't that thrilled with the mini-reunion. We hadn't been that close back then, and I guessed after thirty years we wouldn't have much in common.

Despite my reluctance, I found the morning very enjoyable. Shirley prepared mini-omelets, crepes with fresh strawberries, and an assortment of breakfast rolls to tempt us off our diets. I especially enjoyed becoming re-acquainted with Anne Welklin, whom I remembered only vaguely. Like me, she'd spent her career in law, and we had a lot to talk about. While Shirley and the other woman spoke of golf and quilting, Anne and I discussed the highs and lows of our years in the profession.

Once we caught up on the past, Anne asked, "What made you decide to become a private detective?"

She wasn't the least bit condescending, and I admitted that I liked actually pursuing criminals rather than simply prosecuting them once someone else caught them. "Right now we're looking into the disappearance of a woman who left behind three daughters. Since she doesn't seem the type to do that, I think her boyfriend killed her and hid her body."

"How sad!" Anne said. "Do you have any leads?"

That's what's nice about people who understand the law. They go right from the "too bad" phase to "What are you doing about it?" I explained that the suspect had died in a fall. "Since we can't question him, we have no any idea where to look for her."

Anne straightened her glasses. "I've had similar cases. Usually the body is buried someplace the guy knows well."

"True," I agreed, "but that doesn't make it easier. They lived on a farm, so there's almost two hundred acres this guy knew well."

Folding her arms, Anne thought about that. "I guess my next question would be where had he been spending a lot of time?"

For three hours, the feeling I was neglecting the agency and letting down the Isley girls was only a tickle at the back of my brain. As soon as Anne and Marilyn left, however, I gave Shirley a hug, tossed my overnight bag in the back seat, and headed home.

My phone showed no new messages and no answers to either my voicemails or my texts. As I drove, I focused on home and what I might be missing.

For some reason the cat came to mind. She'd been outside my window again yesterday morning before I left Allport. When I offered chicken with a water chaser she accepted, eating more delicately than before. Still, when I'd tried to pet her, I was rewarded with a snarl. "Okay, Brat," I said. "For now our relationship is unilateral, but someday I expect a little gratitude."

Thoughts of the fiercely independent cat led to thoughts of Pansy Isley. She appealed to me in a way no other child had, and I couldn't say why. She wasn't the type of kid I was at her age, since I'd been more bookworm than animal lover. Still, we shared a sense of right and an unwillingness to keep quiet when wrongs arise. I thought Pansy could become whatever she set her mind to, and I hoped against hope that her mother wasn't dead. If Rose was gone, as I feared, I vowed to see that whoever took charge of Pansy's future recognized her independent spirit as a positive trait, not something to be squelched or shamed to silence.

Along with cats and kids I thought about my sisters, both so busy they hadn't spoken to me all weekend. That didn't happen often these days, and I kept waiting for the phone to ring. In the end I became worried, and I found myself wishing the drive from Flint to Allport didn't take so long.

CHAPTER THIRTY-FIVE

Faye

We made our usual Sunday morning visit to Dale's mom a little earlier than usual. Leaving Buddy in the back seat, we entered the Meadows. Harriet was up and dressed, staring out the window, unaware we were there until Dale spoke to her.

Dale's mom is a woman with no interests these days. Anything she ever enjoyed is beyond her physical abilities. Macular degeneration prevents her from reading. She can't get the hang of audio books because she drifts off and misses large sections of the plot. Television is only a blur of movement, and she has to have the volume up so loud that others complain. We bought her earphones, but she refuses to wear them, claiming they make her look like Ray Walston in My Favorite Martian.

Arthritic hands rule out the crafts Harriet once practiced: knitting, crocheting, and quilting. When she first moved to the Meadows she'd made friends, but everyone she got close to died. Harriet lives on, sitting in her wheelchair, lying on her bed, and wishing her stubborn body would succumb to something fatal.

Dale does his best to be a good son, though the irritating buzzes and bright lights at the Meadows make his head hurt. He entered the room first and went to his mother, touching her gently on the shoulder.

e seldom used my name, even after thirty-three years. To Dale she said, "It's been a long time since you came to see me."

"It's Sunday, Mom," Dale answered. "We always come on Sundays."

"It gets lonely sitting here all the time. I wish you came more often, at least once a week."

Mentioning that I came on Wednesdays and whatever other times she needed something or the staff needed me to intervene wouldn't have done any good. She went on, "I suppose you're working a lot."

Harriet never really grasped the extent of Dale's disability. He looks fine, so she assumes he's completely recovered. The easiest thing to do was go along. "Yes," Dale said. "Always busy."

"Have you worked up on Bois Blanc Island lately?"

Dale glanced at me. Her mind was ten years in the past today, before his accident. "Not for a while."

"Good money up there," she said. "Cutting trees for the tourists."

"Yes," Dale replied. "Good money."

"I wish you came to see me more often. It's lonely just sitting here."

As we drove up US 23, Dale stared out at Lake Huron. Riding in a vehicle, he's most comfortable looking to the side. Facing forward, he tells me, is like being in a fast-moving, 3D video game.

We were quiet for a while. It depressed Dale to hear his mother complain each week, though he knew she was well cared for. Focusing on the least bothersome part of the visit I said, "I'd forgotten that week you went up to Bois Blanc to clear land for a cabin. Odd that your mom remembers it."

"She was impressed that we loaded a truck full of equipment onto the ferry and hauled it up there. It was a pretty big undertaking."

"Not much up there, right?"

"No. They call Bois Blanc 'the other island' because it's the opposite of Mackinac. Lots of nature, lots of quiet, no fudge."

"One of Ben McAdams' friends, Colt Farrell, has a lot up there," I said. "Sheriff Brill looked at satellite images, but there's just trees and a dock."

Too late I realized we were supposed to be taking a break from investigation. I started to apologize, but Dale just chuckled.

"They might use that lot, if Farrell is involved and if whoever attacked you needs a place to hide from the police search going on in Allport. You have to admit, though, we don't even know there is a plot. That missing weapon might just mean some Weekend Warrior has sticky fingers."

I was thrilled by his use of *we*. If Dale took an interest in the agency, he might not be so bored. He futzed in his workshop, fixing small engines, but that gave him little intellectual stimulation. Though it broke my heart to see him watching *Wagon Train* re-runs for the fourth time, I'd despaired of finding things he could do that he wanted to do.

"There's a reason someone stole that weapon, and Barb thinks Farrell is part of it," I said. "He was on the farm twice we know of, hunting for something. The second time there were two men with him. We think it was Ben's card-playing buddies, Stone and Sharky."

"Okay, so McAdams hid the grenade launcher in his bunker after someone stole it from the Guard camp in Grayling. Maybe he didn't tell his friends where it was."

"So they watched the farm, saw me head into the woods by myself, and figured I knew something." I touched the sore spot on my head. "I didn't know as much as they thought, but I stumbled on what they were after."

"How did they know where you were going?" Dale asked. "Did they follow you and your sisters every time one of you left home?"

I frowned. "That doesn't seem likely."

"You said the man who hit you knew you were a detective."

That bothered me, and I lapsed into silence. It was unsettling to think of those men watching me go into the woods, following in hopes I'd do exactly what I did: lead them to the weapon. Whoever had taken the grenade launcher from Ben's bunker needed a new place to hide it now, because the sheriff and the Allport police were searching for it. Where had they taken their prize?

While the new hiding place could be anywhere in Michigan, there was only one spot that we knew was connected to the plotters: Bois Blanc. I decided that tomorrow morning I'd call Rory and see if he could figure out a way for someone to physically check Farrell's lot for the grenade launcher. It would be tricky, since there was no evidence Farrell was involved in anything illegal, but Rory would think of something.

We were nearing Cheboygan, and I asked Dale, "Do you want to find a place to stay here or keep going north to Mackinaw City? We can cross the bridge and visit the casino in St. Ignace if you want."

He was quiet for a few seconds. I was about to ask again when he said, "What if I show you around Bois Blanc?"

"What? Why? I mean—"

"Look, Faye, I know this is supposed to be our time off, but I also know you're dying to see if that gun is hidden on Farrell's property. It won't take long to check out Farrell's lot, and afterward we can sit on the porch of the B&B and watch the sun set over the straits."

CHAPTER THIRTY-SIX

Barb

Around 1:00 p.m. I exited I-75, pulled into a McDonalds, got a coffee at the drive-through window, parked in an angled spot, and called Rory.

"Hi, Barb."

"Hi. How are things in beautiful Allport?"

"Good," he replied. "The weather's going to be great all week, they say."

"That's nice. Have you heard from Faye or Retta since yesterday?"

"Um, yeah. I spoke to both of them, actually."

"Why?"

"Why?"

"Yes, Rory. Why did you speak to my sisters?"

"Well, there were some things about Rose Isley's disappearance we had to clarify. So I talked with Retta."

"And Faye?"

"Right. She was there. With Retta."

"At the house?"

"Um, no. We were at the sheriff's office."

"On Saturday? The sheriff called everyone in on the weekend?"

"Well, we thought it was best if everybody met and put together what we know all at once."

"I see."

"We got some new information, some new leads to track down."

"That's good." I was getting all the wrong vibrations. "Faye sent me a message that sounded kind of weird. Is everything okay up there?"

"Barb, I give you my solemn word, Faye is perfectly healthy. I saw her myself yesterday, and she told me she and her husband were going away for a little R&R."

"Which they never, ever do."

"Well they did. And like I said, Faye's fine. When you two get back together, she'll tell you what she did while you were gone."

I didn't think Rory was lying, but there was a lot he wasn't saying. Promising I'd see him soon, I hung up. Retta and Faye were avoiding me. Rory was holding back. I wouldn't find out what I'd missed until I got home, but once I got there, I'd make them confess all.

CHAPTER THIRTY-SEVEN

Faye

We made some calls from Cheboygan, and for once I was glad Retta had insisted I get a smartphone. With it I located the number of the B&B, and while the rooms there were booked for the night, the woman suggested a second place that allowed small pets. I also found a plat map and located Farrell's property on the northern shore of the island. It took every iota of computer savvy I had, but I didn't want to tell anyone else our plan. No one we know would have approved of Dale and me snooping on our own.

In our defense, we had no intention of doing anything dangerous. We'd drive by the lot. If there was any sign it was occupied, we'd keep going. If it was empty, we'd stop and take a look. Not being police officers, we didn't need a search warrant to do a little spying. If we were caught, we could claim to be tourists who didn't know morel mushroom season had come and gone already.

We were in time for the Bois Blanc ferry's noon run, and we waited patiently for our turn to drive on board.

Buddy, who'd napped in the back seat the whole way, became excited about this new adventure, and I could hardly hear the guide's instructions as we bought our ticket. Once aboard the *Kristen D*, I put Buddy's leash on and led him to the observation area. He was interested in everything, but I kept him close, speaking firmly. If I do that he'll stop barking, though he always pouts a little. He's calling our attention to new things, and he doesn't understand why we don't appreciate the service he provides.

The ferry staff went about their casting-off duties, and then we were under way. Buddy didn't like the ferry horn one bit, but once it went silent, so did he. We watched the Fourteen Foot Shoal Light approach and recede as we headed to open water. The Mackinac Bridge was on our left, and the cars on it looked like bugs heading to and from a picnic.

When we neared the island's dock, Dale and I went back to our vehicle and waited our turn to disembark. Buddy was really excited now, and he bounded from one side of the car to the other, trying to see what everyone was doing. After driving off the ferry we turned left, onto a dirt road. It's funny that there's no pavement on Bois Blanc, which has cars, and pavement on Mackinac Island, which doesn't. Bois Blanc's roads were designated only as good dirt or poor dirt on the plat map.

Soon we came to Pointe aux Pins, the island's largest settlement. Amenities are few on Bois Blanc, but at the general store we found a large paper map of the island. That meant I no longer had to squint at the 2x4-inch image on my phone. As we toured the town Dale told me about the week he'd spent up here. He pointed out a couple of chapels, a community building, a post office, a bar, and what looked like a one-room school.

Leaving the tiny town, we continued west on Lime Kiln Point Road and turned onto Bob Lo Drive, which cut across to the north shore. On our left the land was mostly state forest and it formed a point that leaned west, toward Round Island. Beyond Round Island was the most famous of the three, Mackinac Island. When the lake appeared again ahead of us I turned right, following the road that traced the island's north shore.

We drove on, passing cottages scattered among the trees and occasional signs identifying points of interest. "There are a couple of inland lakes," Dale told me, "but I think they're on the south end."

Half-listening, I searched mailboxes and signposts, looking for something that would tell me we'd reached our destination. We had to be getting close, so I slowed way down. It wasn't like there was traffic to consider.

There was no sign posted, but I stopped when I saw a rickety wooden dock with a sailboat tied to it. Using the binoculars from the glove-box, I took a closer look and saw the name Rory had mentioned: *Mr. A.I.*

Since there wasn't a driveway, I pulled off onto the grass. Dale and I got out, and I opened the back door for

Buddy. I left his leash on, afraid he might run after a rabbit or deer and get lost. He sniffed happily around my feet, taking in new territory he'd no doubt claim for his own.

The view of the water was spectacular, and the spot reminded me of an old poem where the guy says something about peace dropping slow. As the quiet sat on my shoulders, they relaxed. I hadn't even realized they were tense.

On either side of the lot were trees, mostly scrub pine but farther back a few oaks. The smell of evergreens swirled toward us, pushed by a breeze off the water. Along the tree-line wildflowers peeped shyly out, preferring shade to sunlight. There were a few ducks on the water, some with rears up as they searched the bottom for food. Dale touched my arm, pointing upward where a hawk flew above us in a slow arc.

"The deer up here are almost tame," he said softly. "I saw a woman feed one bread out of her hand."

I watched the boat to see if there was anyone aboard. It seemed empty, bobbing gently in the waves that pushed at the shore. Apparently used for fishing, it had a single rod set upright in a holder on the near side.

For a few minutes Dale and I stood enjoying sights and sounds that were not man-made. After a while, we began our search, circling away from each other and weaving slightly to cover more ground. Dale's path led him into the trees, while I crisscrossed the open space.

I'd almost reached the shore when movement on the left caught my eye. Turning, I saw a man coming toward me, fishing tackle in both hands. He wore ratty jeans and an equally worn denim jacket. Pulled low on his forehead was a camp cap pierced with fish-hooks and enameled metal pins. When he got closer, I saw that at least some of them were military.

The guy was walking with his head down, so we saw him first. Buddy started barking, and the man stopped. "Who are you?" he demanded.

Though he wasn't a big man, his manner was threatening. He glared at me, neck stretched toward me and eyes glittering with animosity. His mouth didn't quite close when he finished speaking, and I got a glimpse of what looked like a mouthful of canine teeth. Movie villains came to mind, the kind with no moral boundaries. If I had to describe him in one word, it would have been creepy.

Mushroom hunting didn't explain me walking the shoreline. "I-I was looking for stones," I stammered. "I collect pretty ones."

"On somebody else's property?" he asked harshly. He dropped the creel and pole he carried to the ground and took a step toward me. He had big hands for his size, and I pictured them closing around my neck.

"I didn't realize—"

Buddy stepped in front of me, barking furiously. He heard the threat in the stranger's tone and was more than willing to defend me. The man's hand went to his waistline, and I saw a pistol holstered there.

"Don't!" I cried. "He's on a leash!"

The stranger paused, leaving his hand close to the gun but not on it. "You got no right here," he said, flashing those pointy teeth. "I ought to—"

"Hey, there." Dale's voice came from behind me, and the stranger stepped back. When I turned, Dale was approaching faster than I'd seen him move in years. In one hand he held a stout tree branch. It might have been a walking stick, but the way he carried it made it look like a weapon.

The fisherman's expression changed from malevolent to blank, and the threat I'd felt a few seconds earlier melted away.

"Hey, man," he called to Dale. "How you doing?"

Reaching my side, Dale stopped. "Sorry if we trespassed on your land. It's just such a beautiful view from here."

"No problem," the guy said. "It ain't my land. I was just passing and saw her." He spoke as if I wasn't present or perhaps didn't matter. "I knew she wasn't the owner." He pointed past us. "My place is farther down."

"I see." Dale's tone was doubtful. "All the same, we'll be going." He took my arm, and we started away. I turned several times to look back, afraid he'd pull that gun and shoot us dead.

The guy didn't move. When we got into the car, he was still standing where we left him.

"What was that?" Dale asked in a low tone.

Shaking my head I replied. "He looks like a nut case."

"I thought he was going to attack you."

It was better not to mention the gun. No sense making Dale as scared as I was. Putting the car into gear, I pulled back onto the road. "Quite an over-reaction to seeing people on someone else's land."

Dale sighed. "At least we checked the place out. No sign of a hidden weapon or other anti-government paraphernalia."

I glanced in the rear-view mirror. "Wish we'd got a look at that boat."

We dined on whitefish and fresh asparagus, watched a beautiful sunset, and relaxed in a charming, quiet room. Breakfast was at 6:30 the next morning. Our ferry was scheduled to leave at 9:30, which allowed us enough time to drive past Ferrell's lot again. The boat called *Mr. A.I.* was gone, but we did see a pair of eagles, swooping and rolling over the water in search of prey.

CHAPTER THIRTY-EIGHT

Barb

Retta finally called Monday morning, and I pushed aside my cereal and half-eaten banana. "What's up with Faye?" I asked. "Why did they take off so suddenly?"

She was surprisingly tight-lipped. "She'll tell you about it when she gets home this afternoon." Apparently that was all she had to say on that subject, because she went right on. "I called to ask if the girls could stay at your house for a while."

I haven't often been asked to kid-sit, but the idea appealed to me now. The Isley girls were easy, being old enough to take care of themselves and so close they didn't argue much. "Sure," I said. "They can frost the cookies Faye made yesterday. She must have forgotten them when she got called away to do whatever it is that you won't tell me about." It was a shameless attempt to pick information out of Baby Sister, but for once she refused to share.

"I might be away from my phone for a while, but if you text, I'll get back to you as soon as possible."

"You without your phone? Are you having major surgery?"

"Ha, ha. We're almost there, and I'm going to drop the girls off and go. I'll talk to you later."

It was only a few seconds later that I heard her car stop outside, followed by three doors slamming closed as the girls got out. Typically, she'd asked for a favor assuming I'd agree. I hurried to the door to catch her, but she was already pulling away. Though she waved enthusiastically, she didn't stop.

There were secrets here. Faye had made cookies then went somewhere with Dale for an overnight trip, leaving them in the refrigerator, unfrosted. For Faye, that was unheard of. Retta had to know where Faye had gone and why, but she wasn't willing to share. Now she was off on a mysterious adventure of her own, and I was not privy to those details either.

I thought about pumping the girls for information, but it didn't seem right. After asking casually where Retta had gone and getting a vague answer about errands she had to run, I gave up.

"There are cookies to be frosted," I said, "are you interested?"

Of course they were. I set them up with the tools for the job, and they got busy with icing and sprinkles. Daisy lost interest once she'd frosted two cookies, and she sat down at the kitchen table to eat her creations.

Pansy and Iris were old hands, and while Pansy's work was acceptable, Iris was a cookie decorating master. I stood around for a while, sharing little tidbits about cookies, icing, and such. They seemed interested in learning where vanilla comes from and how food dyes are made for a while, but when they began repeating the same "Cool!" and "Wow!" comments, I left them to their work and went down to the office to check our messages.

As I entered the room I was humming, but I stopped abruptly. Things were different. My space had been invaded.

At one end of my desk was a lamp that looked like it came from the early 1900s, and its mate sat on the bookshelf across the room. Lined up on a shelf were three vases, alike except for size. On each, in silhouette, a frock-coated man offered flowers to a lady in a wide-skirted dress. In the bottom left corner of each window was a small pillow in shades of blue, green, and lilac.

I hated them all on sight.

Here's the thing. I like clear spaces and hard angles in my office. The only place I want softness is on the seat of my chair. The only colors I require are the tones of different woods. Decorative objects are nice in bedrooms and living rooms, but offices are places of business and should, therefore, look businesslike. I went to work putting things back the way they should be.

189

CHAPTER THIRTY-NINE

Retta

I left the girls with Barbara Ann for a while so I could do a little role-playing. I didn't stop because it's hard not to tell Barbara what she wants to know, and right then I had two secrets. Faye had made me promise not to tell about her bad experience, and I was going to go to the River of Fulfilling Life Church to find out what I could about Ben McAdams and who his friends were. When Faye got back, I'd sit down with both of them and compare notes.

I stopped first at the local Salvation Army store. The girls there all know me because I give away really good stuff. One of them told me once that the staff takes what they want from my donation bags before they put the rest out for resale. It isn't quite fair, but I guess if you work somewhere, you get the perks.

Telling them I was shopping for someone else, I chose an outfit I wouldn't otherwise have worn in a million years: a dowdy cotton dirndl skirt, a plain, pale yellow blouse, white crew socks, a knitted beret, and tennis shoes with drops of blue paint on one toe. In the far corner of a large parking lot, I climbed into the back seat and fumbled my way out of my clothes and into the new-old ones. I'll admit I worried a little about how clean they were, but I told myself a detective has to make sacrifices in order to succeed. Next I used a couple of the wipes I keep in my car to take off every bit of makeup I'd put on so carefully that morning. Tucking my hair into the beret, I took off my earrings and bracelets then did something I seldom do. I turned my phone off and after giving it a little caress, hid it in the pocket of the skirt.

A glance in the visor mirror told me I looked dull as dishwater, as Mom used to put it. Leaving the car, I walked the two blocks to the River of Fulfilling Life Church, hoping I didn't see anyone I knew. The entry door was blocked open with a chunk of wood, and inside were five women standing around a large table. Some sort of project was in progress, which was perfect.

The women looked up when I temporarily blocked the light coming in the doorway. Most just looked at me, but one of them smiled. "Hi, there," she called. "Can we help you?"

"My name is Margie," I replied. "I'm new in town, and someone told me this was a good place to meet people."

"It certainly is." The woman stepped forward. "I'm Dee. This is Carrie, and Pam, and Joan, and that's Diane."

"Nice to meet you," I said to the group. "Is the pastor in?"

"It's his day to visit the sick," Dee said. "You're welcome to wait."

"I guess I can stay a few minutes." Gesturing at the table I asked, "Can I help with what you're doing?"

"It's a mission project." I think it was Carrie who spoke. "We're filling packets for a birthing hospital in Ethiopia. Joan makes these cloth backpacks, and we add things the new mothers can take home for themselves and for their babies."

Eagerly they showed me the array of items they'd either made or collected to send overseas. "A nurse who worked at a hospital over there came and spoke to us about the needs they face. We decided to help out."

"It's a Christian hospital," Diane put in.

Picking up a bag, I looked it over. Simply made but sturdy, it had straps that allowed it to be worn as a backpack, freeing the hands. The straps were particularly clever, made from the often useless cloth belts that come with dresses, sweaters, and tops. Thinking of the collection of those I had at home in my closet, I vowed to get them to this woman, who made practical use of something most people toss away.

"The bags are really great, Joan." She didn't reply or even smile, but she gave me a brief nod of acknowledgement.

I was given the task of rolling receiving blankets so they could be stuffed into corners of the packets. Carrie showed me how to place them so they cushioned the other objects and kept them from crashing together.

We talked, as people do when they're engaged in a mutual project. They were nice women, and I began to feel bad about lying to them. It also felt weird to have my phone turned off. Used to having it, I missed the discreet ding every few seconds that lets me know someone is thinking of me.

Since I was already there and the lie had been told, I followed through with my charade. In response to questions I spun a story about moving from Detroit a few weeks before. "My husband wanted out of the city," I told them. "He chose Allport because an old army buddy of his lives on a farm out of town. But something terrible happened. The friend died in an accident a few days ago. Now we don't know anybody."

"Do you mean Ben McAdams?" Pam asked.

I smiled. "Why, yes. He's the one who told us about this church."

"Ben used to come at least twice a week," Carrie said. "But we hadn't seen much of him lately."

"That's funny," I said. "He told us everyone here is real nice and the Word gets preached every Sunday."

Joan looked up from her work as if judging the truth of my statement. Her gaze made me nervous, but after a few seconds, she went back to packaging tiny socks in zip bags.

"I saw Ben at the credit union a couple weeks back," Diane said. "I told him we missed them at church. He said he was busy on the farm. Rose and the girls too."

Joan spoke for the first time, and it sounded like the voice of doom. "I pray he was ready when the Lord called on him to explain how a man can be too busy to come to church."

The other women nodded, and one of them added an "Amen."

When the last backpack was in the shipping box, the pastor still hadn't returned. "I guess I'll come back tomorrow," I told the women. "It was nice meeting everybody."

We left the building as a group, but Dee put a hand on my arm. "Walk with me." She locked the door then pointed east. "I live over there, and it won't take a minute to make us a cup of tea."

Joan hung back, obviously hoping to be invited along, but Dee wished her a good day and turned away. I got the impression Joan wasn't the type people hang around with any more than necessary. Godly, yes, and able to do many things. Just not much fun.

On the other hand, Dee seemed good-humored and upbeat, the kind who doesn't let the shadows of evil in the world block out the rays of sunshine. She grasped my arm. "I'm going to have to lean on you a little," she said. "Got a bum hip, and standing on that tile floor has started it barking at me."

Dee chatted about the neighborhood as we walked the block to her house, a clapboard-sided remnant of the 1950s. In her sunlit kitchen she put the teakettle on, set out two china cups with saucers, and gave me my choice of Earl Grey or Orange Spice tea. Once she poured hot water over the bags and set the kettle back on the stove, she sat down across from me, met my eyes, and asked, "What are you up to, Mrs. Stilson?"

My face burned with embarrassment. Though it had been years since Don's death, my picture had been in the paper plenty of times back then. A hat and glasses might fool some people, but there's always one sharpie who's paying attention.

Something in Dee's forthright manner made me answer honestly. I told her about the detective agency, the farm, and the girls. She listened closely, at first, I think, to see if I was lying, but later with interest in the story.

When I finished, she said, "Those poor girls! Rose is a bit impractical, but she's a good mother. I doubt she'd run off and leave them with Ben." Looking away for a moment she said, "It's a sin to gossip, and the Devil loves it when somebody starts, so I'll tell you only what I saw and heard myself. There's been plenty of talk, but I won't pass that along."

I twitched in my chair. This was what I'd come for, though I wasn't exactly getting it the way I planned.

"I love our church," Dee began. "It's small, and it isn't under the thumb of some national organization that tells us we have to let gay ministers baptize our babies or change the litany to suit somebody's idea of politically correct wording." She gave me a hard look. "God is a He as far as I'm concerned, because that's what the Bible says. And while I have no desire to stone gay people, they don't belong in my church until they stop doing what the Bible tells us is an abomination."

"I understand."

She smiled grimly. "That's your way of saying you disagree, but let's leave it at that. As I said, I like my church, but for the last year or so, we've had some trouble."

"With Ben McAdams?"

"Colt Farrell is the ringleader, but Ben and a few of the men and even some of the women agree with him."

"About what?"

"About women and their place in the world."

Things the girls had said came back to me. "You mean that we're meant to be ruled by men."

Dee pointed an arthritic finger at me. "That's Bible teaching. We are weaker vessels, and we're to submit to our husbands."

I was confused. "If you agree, where does the trouble come in?"

Dee sipped at her tea, shoving the bag she'd left floating in the cup off to one side. "First Colt said women shouldn't get to vote on the church's business. He and his bunch argued it's fairer if one person—a man—represents each family." She set her cup down with a clink. "I don't have a man anymore, so I don't get a vote. I didn't like it, but I told myself I could still voice my opinions."

"But that wasn't enough for them."

"Right." Her lips pursed in anger. "Once it was decided that only the men could vote, Colt said women shouldn't speak out in meetings, either. He found it in the Bible."

"St. Paul, I believe," I said grimly. "I've wanted to discuss that with the man myself."

"If he's in the Bible, God wants us to hear what he had to say." Dee spoke forcefully, but it seemed like she was trying to convince herself as much as me. "Last month Colt said women shouldn't hold leadership positions in the church. We shouldn't even sit on committees, according to him."

"Did he get his way?"

"Not yet, but he isn't the kind to give up."

"Is that why Ben left the church?"

She shook her head. "I don't know why they stopped attending. It's a shame for Rose and the girls, but at least Colt isn't as mouthy without Ben to support him. Floyd tosses in an 'Amen' every time he speaks, but people know Floyd just wants someone to blame for everything that's gone wrong in his life." She sipped her tea again. "Going to services used to be a joyful hour of communion with the Lord and other loving hearts. Now Colt starts his lecturing and I have to fight down the urge to make trouble."

"Don't some of the men stand up for the women?"

She nodded. "They do, but to be honest, we can barely afford to pay the pastor and keep up the building. Being a big financial contributor, Colt usually gets his way in the end." She raised her cup but forgot it halfway to her mouth. "He's Joan's husband."

"Joan's last name is Farrell?"

"Yes. She and Colt own an electronics store on 10th."

"What does Joan think of his views?"

"She agrees a hundred percent." Dee turned the teakettle on again. "Joan grew up living on welfare peanut butter and venison shot at midnight. Colt provides a good living, so she thinks the sun rises and sets on his say-so."

I tried to recall the names of the men who were at the farm the night Ben died. "Is there anyone at your church named Sharky?"

She thought about it. "No."

"Could it be a nickname for one of the men?"

"If it is, I don't know it," Dee said. "I call people by their proper names unless they ask me not to."

I liked that. I have a perfectly good name, Margaretta, but my parents called me Retta from Day One. I learned to accept it, though Retta doesn't have half the music Margaretta does. Since I'm not fond of my own nickname, I don't usually use them.

"No one went out there when Ben stopped coming to church?"

Dee shrugged. "I guess we were all afraid he'd think we were sticking our noses into his business." Putting a hand over her mouth as if to stop herself from saying more, she said it anyway. "Ben didn't like people questioning what he said and did. If Rose objected to anything, he'd say God told him it had to be that way. She got tired of hearing that."

"And you think they quarreled about it?"

"She tried not to argue in front of the girls. She didn't want them scared." Dee's smile was sad. "She really does think men are supposed to lead the family, but I think she was afraid of the choices Ben might make for her girls."

Like taking them out of school? I thought. Or giving one of them to his friend? That was especially creepy.

"I guess she'll have other things to worry about when she gets back home," Dee said. "Any idea when that will be?"

"No. I mean, I haven't heard anything." Thanking Dee for the tea and the information, I headed for my car, hoping she hadn't seen the doubt in my eyes. Barbara was very likely right: Rose Isley was never coming home, and it broke my heart.

Many things went through my mind, but I forced myself to concentrate on just one. Though my fears for Rose were deep, there was nothing I could do for her at the moment. The girl-haters' club at Ben's church was irritating, but I didn't see how it connected to the theft of a grenade-gun from the National Guard.

I wanted to contact the men Dee had mentioned, to see if they really were crazy enough to steal a weapon from the U.S. government and plot some terrible use for it. I wanted to know more about Colt Farrell's views, but interviewing a man like him wasn't something a woman could do effectively. Taking out my phone, I turned it on and located Gabe Wills in my contacts.

"You want me to buy electronics where?" Gabe said when I explained the job.

"Mr. A.I. It's the name of a store in the Morton Plaza. What I really want is for you to engage the owner in conversation."

"Engage?"

I sighed. "I want you to talk with him, Gabe. About religion."

"Religion?"

Holding back a sigh, I answered a dozen questions from "What if the owner isn't the one who waits on me?" to "What if he doesn't believe in Jesus?" Finally I said, "Gabe, if I'm right about this guy, all you have to do is say you and your wife are looking for a church. That will get his interest."

"Um, Mrs. Stilson..."

"Yes?"

"I can't tell him my wife wants a church. I don't have a wife."

"Okay. Say it's your girlfriend."

He thought about that. "I guess that's okay."

It was apparently all right to lie about looking for a church but not about whether he was married. Gabe's reasoning escaped me, but I was happy he agreed to do it. Barbara wouldn't approve, but if Gabe got Farrell talking, we'd get an idea of his level of craziness. It might even shed light on what they were planning to do with the grenade-thingy.

By the time Gabe arrived twenty minutes later, I'd changed into my own clothes again. With specific instructions: "Look interested and don't argue," I sent him inside. Gabe isn't capable of debating Biblical doctrine, but his look of constant confusion might generate a desire to instruct in a pompous sort like Farrell.

Twenty minutes later, Gabe left the store, arms laden with items I agreed to pay for in exchange for his help. I met him at his truck, but first he had to show me what he'd bought, like a kid at Christmas. Once we got that out of the way, I led him through his meeting with Colt Farrell.

"Well, he didn't wait on me at first," Gabe began. "He was on the phone in the back. When he finally came out, I mentioned about my girlfriend and me looking for a church home. That's what they call it." Gabe's tone was instructive. "A church home. The guy was real excited to tell me about his church."

"What did he say?"

Gabe's grin was wide. "Let's just say Ms. Evans would have him for lunch."

"I understand he isn't a fan of women leading in church."

"Women leading anything, anyplace, anytime." Gabe sniffed. "I got a big lecture on the downfall of the great U.S. of A. and how it all started when we gave women the vote."

"Did it, now."

He raised his hands in comic defense. "Don't blame me! I'm just telling you what he said. According to Mr. Farrell, there's indistutable proof that every state in the U.S. started falling apart the minute it let women vote."

I didn't correct Gabe's mistaken version of indisputable, though Barbara certainly would have.

"He says it was a woman who put the information all together, so that proves it's true."

Sure it does. "Is he the type who might get violent on the subject?"

Gabe's eyes widened. "Heck, yeah! He started out pretty tame, but the more he talked, the madder he got. He said it's women's fault we got a welfare state and Muslims taking over and illegal aliens sneaking across the borders by the millions."

"How did we do that?"

"That wasn't real clear." Gabe scratched his chin. "He did say they got no right being in Congress or running anything."

"Because our heads are stuffed with cotton, hay, and rags."

"What?"

"Never mind. How did you get away from all that wisdom?"

"I was starting to get a little antsy about that." Gabe pushed a lock of greasy-blond hair out of his eyes. "His phone rang. I already paid for my stuff, so I told him, 'Go ahead and take the call.' I wanted to get out of there before he started in again."

I pressed an extra twenty into his hand. "I'm so glad you helped with this, Gabe."

He stuffed the bill in his jeans pocket. "Is this a case the Smart Detectives are working on?"

"It didn't begin that way," I replied, "but I'm pretty sure it is now."

CHAPTER FORTY

Faye

When Dale and I got home, Barb's car was in the driveway and the Isley girls were in the back yard. Iris lay on the porch swing, her legs draped over one end as she read a book. Daisy rushed forward to hug me as we got out of the car. Seconds later she and Buddy were playing catch with a tennis ball.

Barb came onto the porch, shading her eyes from the bright sun. "Retta's on some mission, so I'm kid-sitting. Pansy took Styx for a walk, which is a good thing." She gestured at Buddy, joyfully chasing down the ball. "I'll have her take him out to the workshop when they get back so he and Buddy don't meet."

"Good."

Barb backed into the kitchen, her eyes moving from me to Dale and back. "So what's going on?"

"Let's sit down, and we'll tell you all about it."

"Okay." She lifted one brow in wry amusement. "I just happen to have some newly-frosted sugar cookies, if you're interested."

Dale chose a purple-sprinkled cookie and left, guessing I was about to be scolded. When he closed the door, Barb gave me a little smile to show she wasn't angry. She'd obviously been worried, but I was all right. Now she wanted to know why she'd been kept in the dark.

Once again I told the story of discovering the grenade launcher, getting locked in the bunker, and being rescued by my sons. "We all sat down in Sheriff Brill's office and tried to figure it out," I finished. "Afterward, Rory suggested Dale and I get away for a while, to kind of decompress."

Barb shook her head, disgusted. "I called Rory last night. He didn't lie to me, but he didn't tell the whole truth."

With a sigh I confessed, "I asked Rory—and ordered Retta—not to tell you anything. I didn't want you to worry."

She leaned toward me. "Faye, don't be that much of an idiot ever again, okay? No matter what's going on, I'd much rather know than be left in the dark." She turned aside, and I saw tears in her eyes. "I should have been here."

"Don't start that," I ordered. "That's what Dale said, and it's just silly. Things happen. You and I talked about this, remember?"

Barb sighed. "I know. Just promise me you won't keep things from me ever again."

"Okay. I'm sorry." I paused. "There's more to tell. Dale and I went up to Bois Blanc Island and searched Farrell's lot."

"What?"

I told her about our decision to visit the island, seeing the boat named *Mr. A.I.,* and about meeting the scruffy man on the beach.

"Sharky." Barb told me about Pansy's call saying she'd seen him drive by the house on Saturday.

"If he was here, it wasn't Sharky who hit me."

"No, but whoever did might have given Sharky the grenade launcher to hide up on Bois Blanc."

"We didn't find it on the lot, but it could have been on the boat."

"And we have no idea where the boat is."

We went over everything again but got no further. In the end, we sat sipping our tea and wiping away cookie crumbs. Finally I said, "I should start figuring out what to make the girls for lunch."

"You don't need to walk in the door and start cooking," Barb said firmly. "I'll order pizza."

While she was on the phone Retta bustled in, full of news about her morning. Dale came inside, got two more cookies, and made himself scarce, since her chirpy voice and constant movement puts his nerves on edge. The three of us sat down at the kitchen table, and Retta told us what she'd learned about Ben McAdams and his friends.

Barb was furious at such thinking. "Women are ruining the country? Do they know—?"

"We know, Barbara," Retta interrupted before she could begin a lecture on the contributions of the female sex to society. "We aren't going to debate them, but if they're planning something involving that nasty weapon, we have to stop them."

"I wish we knew where that thing is." Barb glanced around the room as if it might be behind the refrigerator or under the sink.

"At least one of those men must live within the city limits," I said. "Rory will have jurisdiction."

"I looked it up on my phone," Retta said. "Both Stone and Farrell live in the city limits."

"Ben's remote location is probably why the weapon was stored at the farm."

"Do you think they'll give up now that he's dead?" I asked.

"No." Barb was typing search terms into her iPad. "They're probably refiguring things as we speak."

"How are we going to find out what they're planning?"

Barb leaned back in her chair, pinching her lower lip. "We know there's a boat involved. Maybe we should concentrate on that."

"Barbara Ann, Michigan is almost surrounded by water." Retta's tone was disgusted. "The fact that they have a boat tells us *nada*."

Barb's face twitched with irritation. "This is what we do, Retta. We gather scraps of information, put them together in different ways, and see what fits. If they plan to use Farrell's boat for something, we need to know when and why."

The office phone rang, and Barb rose quickly. "I'll get it. You rest." Despite her concern, I followed her down the hallway to listen. Not to be left out, Retta tagged along.

"Yes, Gabe." ... "Good to hear your voice, too." She rolled her eyes at Gabe's exaggerated politeness. As she listened, though, her expression turned dark.

"No, Mrs. Stilson didn't tell us you were helping with our case, but she's here now. I'll put you on speaker so we can all hear what you have to say."

The pizza guy had just pulled up out front. Retta's face flushed, but she covered it by going to the door, taking three large boxes from the sandy-haired kid, and setting them on a side table, all without looking at either of us.

Barb pressed a key, and Gabe's nasal voice came through. "Well, I remembered something the guy at the store said that might be important. He got the call I told Mrs. Stilson about, so I was about to leave then I saw this really cool physical activity monitor he's got in there. They keep track of everything, but Mindy says—"

"Gabe, you had something to tell us about Mr. Farrell."

"Yeah, right. I stopped to look at the monitor—It's really cool—and I heard him say, "I'll take care of that. It'll be harder with two, but we can do it. No more calls. Meet me on the dock at one."

Barb glanced at Retta and me. We both shrugged. The information seemed to confirm the boat was involved, but it might be nothing more than a fishing trip.

"Thanks, Gabe. I'll pass the information on to Chief Neuencamp."

"Okay." After a pause he said, "If you're going after these guys, I can come along. I been practicing with my knife, and I'm getting pretty good at hitting a target."

"You are not to carry any kind of weapon while working for us, Gabe, especially since you're still on probation."

"It's just a jackknife," he said. "Legal, but if I throw it—"

Barb rolled her eyes again. "There will be no knife-throwing. All we're going to do is tell the chief what we know. The authorities will handle it from here."

When she hung up, Barb left her hand on the receiver as if holding onto something would keep her from flying into a rage. "Retta, you sent Gabe to interview a suspect?"

She blushed again, but being Retta, defended herself. "Who was I supposed to get to do it? Rory? Dale? I knew a guy like Farrell would say more to a man than he ever would to one of us."

With a sigh that said she couldn't win, Barb tried to explain. "These aren't games, Retta. Farrell might be part of a group with plans to kill people. Gabe is nobody's idea of an undercover operative. Who knows what Farrell might do to protect himself?"

Retta waved the argument away as if swatting at a fly. "A guy buying new ear buds isn't going to trip Farrell's radar. And like I said, it isn't like Lars is around to help."

Lars Johannsen, Retta's FBI boyfriend, lives in New Mexico. Gabe is about as far from Lars in appearance and brainpower as any two men can get, but she had a point. Gabe had apparently been successful in getting Farrell to share his views.

I knew I should support Barb, but I felt my body temperature start to rise. Nothing brings on a hot flash faster than an argument. "Gabe's not equipped for undercover work, Retta. We want to give him work, but we don't let him investigate."

"You exposed him to danger," Barb said harshly, "without consulting Faye or me first."

"He got the information, didn't he?" Retta's voice vibrated with the bratty tone that irritates Barb no end. "That proves he can handle himself. And I paid him myself, so it didn't have anything to do with the Smarty-pants Detective Agency."

She emphasized the last few words, underscoring her dislike for the name we gave our business. Several times she has proposed her choice, the Sleuth Sisters. Every time, Barb shoots her down.

"The Smart Detective Agency is made up of your sisters." Barb also emphasized the name, underscoring its permanence. "You don't think it might reflect on us?"

"I don't see how." If she doesn't want to acknowledge something, Retta simply ignores it. "How could they possibly know we sent Gabe into their store?"

"You sent him," Barb said. "We didn't. But think about it. If your little charade at the church didn't fool Dee, someone else might have recognized you too. What if one of those women tells Farrell you were asking about Ben? What if she knows Margaretta Stilson is my sister, or Faye's sister—"

"That's a lot of ifs, Barbara." Retta took up the pizza boxes she'd set on the table.

"And another thing," Barb said. "Stop decorating my office for me. I like it plain!"

Looking around, Retta gave one of her ladylike sniffs. "I'm sure it suits you perfectly, Barbara Ann. Now let's call the girls in to eat before their lunch gets cold." She stalked off to the kitchen, leaving Barb fuming with frustration.

"I'll talk to her later," I said. "You'd better update Rory."

Giving them a little cooling-off time was the best I could do. Retta and Barb stop listening to each other early on in any disagreement. It was up to me to get Retta to promise to leave Gabe out of her undercover enterprises and beg her to consult us before beginning the next one.

At the same time, I'd make Barb admit that Retta had gained valuable information. Colt Farrell and the guy I'd seen on the beach at Bois Blanc, probably Sharky, were looking more and more like McAdam's partners in some scheme. The fact that it involved a grenade launcher made it imperative we find out more.

As for Retta redecorating Barb's office, I'd leave that one alone. My opinion was squarely in the middle, but I wasn't about to voice it to either Ms. Plain-and-Simple or Mrs. Spice-it-up.

Entering the kitchen a few minutes later Barb said, "Rory's not answering. I'll try again in half an hour."

Retta had set paper plates and napkins on the patio table at the side of the house, and she was busily serving up slices. By tacit consent, the argument was relegated to the past. Our parents had insisted mealtimes be peaceful, and we continued that way, despite any disagreements we might have before or after.

I called to Iris to fetch Dale and her sisters. Daisy came in first with Buddy at her heels. Dale came next, wiping grease from his hands with a rag. Iris went to look for Pansy and Styx, and everyone present was served by the time she returned, holding the dogs' leash. "I found him fastened to a fencepost down the street," she said, her face pale. "But I can't find Pansy anywhere."

CHAPTER FORTY-ONE

Barb

Iris led me to the spot where she'd found Styx, but there was no sign of Pansy. Had they kidnapped her? Had she been told some lie that made her go voluntarily? I fought to banish images rising in my mind: Pansy in Sharky's hands. Pansy terrified. Pansy sobbing in fear. Pansy dead.

Events of the last few days replayed in my mind. Pansy's stoic acceptance of all she'd faced. Her insightful observations of the adults around her and their motivations. Her sense of humor, a little sarcastic, like mine. How do parents of kidnapped children keep from going mad?

I went all the way to Main Street, around a three-block section, and back home. I asked everyone I met if they'd seen a little blond girl with colored streaks in her hair. No one had.

There was no sign of Pansy in the park. She wasn't at the Dairy Queen—not that I suspected her of running off to get ice cream. She wasn't in any of the stores I passed, nor down the side streets. I turned toward home. My phone was there, buried somewhere in my purse. I had to call Rory, had to get help.

"Here she is! She's back!" Iris' voice betrayed relief.

I hurried to the back porch to see Pansy coming across the yard. I ran toward her, but when I got close, embarrassment overcame me and I stopped short. "We were worried."

Her chin jutted, and I realized Pansy thought she was in trouble. "It's all right. It's just that when we couldn't find you, we were afraid something had happened."

She looked toward the street. "Something did happen, but not to me. I was walking Styx, and I saw him."

"Who?" Retta and Faye came up behind us. I'd been about to ask whom she'd seen, but I was too interested in Pansy's answer to grouse about Faye's less grammatical who.

"Sharky. He was sitting across the street from your house, listening to you talk."

"What do you mean?"

Pansy paused, collecting her thoughts. "Styx and I were coming back from our walk, and I noticed a guy sitting in this junky car in front of the blue house kitty-corner from yours."

"The Partons," Retta supplied, as if it mattered.

"The guy was just sitting there, staring at your house and listening to something that was playing on a laptop. I tied Styx to the fence and sneaked up behind him. When I got close, I saw it was Sharky. He was listening to you all arguing about someone named Gabe."

"Eavesdropping," I said.

"From across the street?" Retta was doubtful. "How could he—?"

"Electronic eavesdropping, Retta."

Her eyes went wide. "Oh!"

I returned my attention to Pansy. "Then what happened?"

She blushed. "I wasn't careful enough. Sharky saw me and took off. I chased him as far as I could, but he got away."

"You chased him?" I was horrified.

"You said it was important to find him!" Pansy looked at me earnestly. "You said you needed my help."

Though Retta pressed her lips together, what she was thinking came out anyway. "I guess I'm not the only one enlisting assistance from underqualified investigators."

"I didn't—" I gave up halfway through the sentence. There was no way I'd convince Retta there was a difference between what I'd said to Pansy and what she'd asked Gabe to do.

When I finally reached Rory, I only gave him a little bit of a hard time about holding out on me. Admitting Faye can be persuasive, I let him off the hook. "Some important things have happened since we last met," I told him. With uncharacteristic honesty I added, "And I'd like to see you."

"That's good to hear, Barb," he said, his tone low. "Let's start with dinner, and we'll go from there."

We'd become less shy about meeting in public. Anyone in Allport who took an interest in our private lives knew we were an item. At first I'd fretted about people saying our agency was too close to the local cops, but Rory argued people will say what they say. "Grownups ignore gossip and get on with their lives," he insisted. I replied that he obviously hadn't grown up with a mother who asked, "What will people think?" at least once a day.

Telling myself Rory's view was better than Mom's, I tried to ignore the whispers behind my back, the speculations about why I never married, and the surprise that I was having a love affair at fifty-three. It wasn't easy, but I was trying.

Rory waited for me outside the restaurant where we first met, our sentimental favorite. The waitress seated us in a corner and asked what we wanted, though she could probably have ordered for him. Rory likes the whitefish, fried, with fries and coleslaw on the side. The man's trim appearance defies logic.

After I told him everything, including how mad I was at Retta, Rory chuckled. "Nobody can accuse your sister of sloth."

Unwrapping my silverware from my napkin, I laid the pieces where they belonged. "I can think of some other deadly sins she's guilty of, pride being prominent among them. Because of her goofy idea, Farrell might realize we suspect him of being in on what McAdams was plotting."

"I don't think you can blame Retta for all of it," Rory countered. "If Pansy's right and Sharky had listening equipment, they've been keeping track of you before today."

"Farrell!" I said. "He owns an electronics store, and he's been in my office." Colt Farrell's visit seemed sinister now, where before I'd deemed it merely irritating. "As soon as I get home, I'm going to find the bug he planted while he was there."

"Why would he do that?" Rory asked.

I counted my arguments on my fingers. "Ben disappeared, and they didn't know where the weapon was. Whatever they're plotting is imminent. Farrell learned Ben's landlords run a detective agency, and he figured we'd be able to track Ben down. Pretending to be a concerned friend, he tried to hire us, but he gave me the creeps and I turned him down. That didn't matter, because he brought along insurance—a listening device he planted in my office." Anger coursing through me I added, "He's heard everything we said for days!"

"Maybe not," Rory replied. "If this Sharky character was listening in his car, it's likely their device transmits just a short distance."

"So they heard us when one of them was close enough to eavesdrop, but that's all."

"Yes."

The waitress came with our food, and we waited until she placed it, stood back, and expressed her wish that we enjoy our meal. When she was gone I said, "That explains how they knew they should follow Faye to the cabin."

"Easier than trying to find the place themselves. All they had to do was wait until she located the weapon and take it."

We ate a little, but neither of us was in the mood to linger over dinner. When I finished half my meal, I set the napkin beside my plate. "If I find a device, should I bring it to your office?"

Rory chuckled. "No need. I'm coming with you."

"We won't be able to prove Farrell planted it even if we find one," I said grumpily.

"We might tie the device to Farrell," Rory said, "but you're right. So far all the evidence we have points to Sharky."

"And we don't know who he is or where he is."

"We're a little closer, thanks to Sheriff Brill. He called that Guard colonel back and had him ask his people about Sharky as a nickname. A Richard Stark from Allport was on duty the weekend the weapon went missing. He and Ben served in the same unit when they were both full-time soldiers, so they've known each other for years. And his sergeant says Stark has a mouthful of pointy teeth, which might get a guy nicknamed Sharky, right?"

"Right." I rose from my chair. "Let's see if we can find that bug."

Rory followed me to the house, where we went right to my office and began a search. At first we found nothing, but he encouraged me to replay Farrell's visit in my mind and recall the things he'd touched. My gaze went to the pencil cup. Farrell had picked it up, ostensibly to read the quotation written on it, but now I suspected a different motive. Dumping the whole thing on my desk, I stood back as Rory sorted through the pencils, pens, and the odd paper clip with his own pen. There it was, a small device that looked a little like Grandma Harriet's hearing aid. Rory wrapped it in some tissues from the box on my desk and put it into his shirt pocket, and I felt a little less violated. Colt Farrell and his buddies wouldn't know what our next move was going to be. But then, neither did we.

CHAPTER FORTY-TWO

Dale and I were watching TV in the den when Barb came home. I heard her voice and Rory's deeper one coming from the office. When he left Barb went upstairs, but she didn't settle down for a long time. I think sometimes that clever mind of hers refuses to quit and let her sleep. I've heard her leave in her car after midnight and come back hours later. When I asked her about it, she said she drives around until she feels tired. What is it she thinks about so much that she can't sleep?

I learned the cause of that night's sleeplessness the next morning when Barb told me she and Rory had found a bug in the office. That made me feel like spiders were walking on my neck. Why had someone done that? What had they heard? Even the most innocent comments I'd made seemed ill-advised at the thought that someone had been skulking outside our home, listening.

Barb and Rory were determined to find Sharky if possible. Since they had that covered, I offered to find out what I could about Floyd Stone. He worked for the post office, so I'd begin there.

The people at the Allport Post Office are cheerful, helpful, and efficient. Cheryl, the postmistress, knows me pretty well, since I do most of the mailings for the agency. I waited until other customers had been served then asked about Floyd Stone.

"He's one of our carriers." Checking the clock she said, "He'll be back around four if you need to speak with him."

"Actually, I wanted your impression of him."

Her unusually high brow tightened. "Is he suspected of a crime?"

I equivocated a little. "Not at this time. I'd just like to know what kind of person he is."

Cheryl thought about it. "I guess he's okay. I mean, we'll never be friends, Floyd and me. He has some pretty weird ideas."

"I've heard that. Can you give me an example?"

She fiddled with the various hand stamps at her work station for a few seconds, lining them up like little soldiers. "Two years ago, the postmaster position opened, and Floyd and I both applied for it. He made it clear he was going to get it, said they'd never choose a woman over a man."

"But you got the job." When Cheryl merely shrugged I went on, "How did he take that?"

"He never said a word." Setting her elbows on the counter, she leaned toward me. "For almost two full months, he didn't say one word to me. I'd tell him things he needed to know; he'd grunt. It was ridiculous." She took a deep breath, as if reliving a decision she'd made. "One day I faced him down. I said, 'Floyd, I know you're disappointed you didn't get the job, but if you can't handle working for a woman, I'll get you transferred to a different office."

"Can you do that?"

She chuckled. "I have no idea, but I couldn't stand his Poor Me face one more day."

"Did it work?"

She waggled a hand in a maybe/maybe not gesture. "He speaks to me if he has to, but that's as far as it goes. Most of the time he avoids me like the plague."

"Great working conditions!"

"Well, he's out on the route all day, so it isn't too bad." She stood up straight again, signaling she needed to get back to work. "I still get little hints he's unhappy, though. A few weeks ago Floyd said he'd heard about a conference I should go to. I took it to mean he thinks I need instruction."

"A conference?"

"On leadership." Cheryl smiled grimly. "I try to look at it as a positive thing. At least he's finally thinking of me as the leader around here."

CHAPTER FORTY-THREE

Barb

Sheriff Brill called the office just before noon. "Did you hear we've got a lead on Sharky?"

"Rory mentioned it, but I don't know the details."

"Richard Stark, National Guardsman, lives in a rental house just outside the city limits. He worked as a janitor at a nursing home until 2013, but he got fired. According to his former boss, a Mrs. Andrews, he spent most of his shifts hiding instead of mopping. No indication of any present employment."

"Mrs. Andrews fired him?"

"She says she never would have hired him in the first place, but the facility administrator has a soft spot for vets and wanted to give him a shot."

"What was the reason for her initial dislike?"

He chuckled. "She says he looked at her funny."

"Not funny in a humorous sense."

"No. He's creepy, she says. If he'd done his work, she'd have tolerated him, but the staff kept finding him sleeping in closets and smoking outside the back door. After the required rigmarole of warnings and documentation, she let him go."

We'd told Brill about the man Faye saw on Bois Blanc, and he reported what he'd done about it. "We sent men to search Farrell's lot, but if the weapon was ever there it's gone now."

I told him what Faye had learned about Floyd Stone at the post office, ending with, "Ben was angry because Rose wouldn't marry him and legitimize their relationship. Stone got passed over for promotion in favor of a woman. And Sharky got fired from his last job by a woman. Three of the four men we're looking at have reason, at least in their own minds, to hate a woman."

"Which could easily become women in general, if you're looking for someone to blame for your problems."

"Exactly. What does Sharky have to say for himself?"

"We can't find him." Brill sounded disgusted. "I sent a car to his place, but it looks like he hasn't been there for several days. There was a dog chained near the front door, and the poor thing was half-dead from thirst. My guys took it to the Humane Society."

"Sharky's gone into hiding?"

"He'll guess we can tie him to the stolen weapon, and he knows Pansy saw him at your house. He'll probably leave the state."

"Unless they plan to complete what they see as their mission first," I murmured. "Sheriff, are there any upcoming events in the area that relate to feminism or women's rights?"

I heard pages flip and guessed Brill was consulting a calendar. "We've got President Bahn coming to the college on the third."

A few weeks before it had been all Retta could talk about. A local woman spent a year in Asia in the 1990s, living with a family whose daughter was her age. Twenty years later the daughter, now Madame Bahn, was president of her country. Currently visiting the US, she was on her way from D.C. to the West Coast and had arranged to stop briefly in Allport to see her old friend. When they heard about it, the local college had asked Madame Bahn to speak while she was in town, and she agreed.

"That could be it," Brill said. "She's a female in a leadership position. They might try to disrupt her speech or even kill her."

"How depraved does one have to be to plan something like that?" I asked, but it was a rhetorical question. I'm only too familiar with the things people do to other people.

"It's time to call in the State Police," Brill said. "It's a credible threat, and the sooner they're on it, the better."

"Thanks, Sheriff. If there's anything we can do, please let us know."

CHAPTER FORTY-FOUR

Retta

We were having an amazing stretch of weather for a
Michigan May. The temperatures went up to the mid-70s
each day, and the rains, which had been plentiful in April,
receded most mornings by 9:00, leaving the world fresh
and green but the ground dry. I stayed away from the
agency for a few days, letting Barbara Ann get over her
grump. I should know better than to try to help, because
she simply cannot admit she might need advice. One good
thing about her is she doesn't hold a grudge. Once she's
said her piece and had a little time to herself, she's fine.

The girls and I had a good time except for two things.
First, Pansy worried about her animals. She kept asking if
Faye's sons knew about reindeer and whether they'd
remember they need a fan when the weather starts getting
hot. Being an animal lover myself, I understood how hard
it was for her to trust someone else to take as good care of
her critters as she had.

The other problem was Daisy, who'd left her doll
behind at the cabin. We assured her Miss Gladiolus was

safe out there, but she worried the doll would think she'd been abandoned. "She always sleeps with me," she explained. "I've got Pansy and Iris to sleep with now, but Miss Gladiolus hasn't got anybody."

To relieve their minds, I decided to take the girls out to the farm for an afternoon. When I called Faye, she said she'd meet us out there. She wanted to see her sons and her horses, of course, but I was a little surprised when Barbara said she'd go as well. She even offered to bring lunch, which meant it would come from somewhere like the Colonel's. Barbara has as much interest in cooking as I have in learning Mandarin Chinese.

We arrived at about the same time, so a small crowd descended on what Bill and Carla have begun calling Prospero's Farm, I guess because it's a magical place.

Pansy was out of the car almost before I turned off the engine, heading for the barnyard. Iris helped Daisy out, promising they'd fetch the doll right after lunch, and headed for the garden, where Carla was thinning a row of carrot plants. Always helpful, Iris knelt at the opposite end of the row and began working.

Daisy was thrilled when Faye opened the back door of her Escape to release Buddy. She squealed his name, and the dog ran to her in an odd little lope in which his back legs looked like they were trying to pass his front ones. Styx was still on his leash, and I held on, fearful of fireworks between the two dogs. Oddly, Buddy completely ignored Styx, and Styx didn't approach Buddy either.

When I unclipped his leash he ran happily off to visit the reindeer.

I recalled Faye telling me that when dogs meet on neutral territory they often tolerate each other better. She might have been right, though the animosity wasn't Styx's fault. The whole problem could have been avoided completely if Faye's dog was a little less grouchy.

Bill came from a shed, calling hellos to everyone. Barbara and Faye unloaded bags and boxes of food, setting them on an old table Cramer had rescued from the donation pile for use at our picnic. It was draped with an old sheet, and Carla had already set out china plates and metal cutlery for everyone (no paper products or plastics for them!) Barb took an oversized jug of water out of the back of her car, and I heard ice cubes click against each other. Bill and Carla frown on soda and other sweet drinks, so water and green tea would be the libations of the day.

As Faye and I set out the food, Barbara and Cramer disappeared into the bunkhouse. Bill gave Pansy a tour of the barnyard, introducing her to Anni-Frid and Agnetha. Pansy came back impressed. "They're beautiful!"

"If you like, you can ride them," Faye told her. "They need exercise, and I'm not up to it."

"Could I?" Pansy asked.

"Sure. Their former owner tossed in their equipment. Between us I think we can figure out how it goes together."

"Can I do it now?"

Faye smiled. "Let's eat first, before everything gets warm or cold or whatever it isn't supposed to be."

Carla and Iris stopped their work and washed their hands at the spigot beside the water trough. Bill and Pansy joined them, while I passed my hand sanitizer to everyone else. Soon we were seated on the grass, munching on chicken, coleslaw, and mashed potatoes, except for Carla, who is vegetarian. She ate something she'd made with tofu.

Bill asked the girls questions about how the place had been run. Iris and Pansy answered, warming to him as he revealed a genuine interest in their opinions. He thought one of the cattle might have a bad leg, and Pansy promised gravely to have a look at it. Carla asked Iris if she thought there were enough vegetables planted to sell at the farm market, and Iris explained how her mother had made successive plantings so crops came in all summer and into the fall. "I can help if you want," she offered. "It's a lot of work."

Carla smiled. "We're new at this, so we keep wondering if we're forgetting steps or doing things we'll be sorry for later."

"Mom has a book," Pansy volunteered. "She keeps track of what she does so the next year she knows what worked and what didn't."

"If you could show it to me, that would be great," Carla said. "After we're finished eating, of course."

"We have to go get Miss Gladiolus," Daisy reminded us. "We can't forget her again!"

"And who is that?" Bill asked.

"She's my doll. Momma made her for me and—" Daisy's eyes filled with tears. "Now I don't know where Momma is and I don't have Miss Gladiolus either."

Faye moved toward Daisy, but Carla was closer and got there first. Taking the child into her arms, she hugged her. "We'll find your doll, Sweetie, don't worry. And wherever your momma is, we all know she loves you very, very much."

A cloud of sadness dimmed our happy picnic for a few moments. Iris looked at her plate. Pansy blinked back her own tears, and the rest of us fell silent. Berating myself for bringing the girls out here and reminding them of their trouble, I struggled for something encouraging to say. Nothing came to mind.

In all likelihood the girls were alone in the world. The farm that had been their home for three years was now in someone else's hands. Their fate would soon be decided by a court system too overwhelmed to consider their wishes. They could keep hoping their mother would return, but hope wasn't enough.

Clearing his throat, Bill said, "Tell you what. Iris can show Carla where Rose's book on growing things is. Pansy can come with me and see about the cow's leg. Mom, Aunt Barb, and Aunt Retta can take Daisy to the cabin to get Miss Gardenia—"

"Miss Gladiolus," Daisy corrected. I thought from Bill's expression he made the mistake on purpose to distract her from her grief.

"Miss Gladiolus. Later we can have some of the honey ice cream Carla conjured up this morning, and then we'll see about riding the horses. Does that sound like a good plan for the afternoon?"

Everyone agreed it was a good plan, and the sadness dissipated a little. "Buddy!" Daisy called, rising and slapping her thighs. "Come on, Bud. We're going for a walk."

CHAPTER FORTY-FIVE

Barb

Though Bill and Cramer hadn't been there long enough to make any substantive changes, the farm seemed somehow livelier. Of course spring wakes everything up, and the crops that former tenants had planted and nurtured were growing nicely. Along with the garden plants, Mom's flowers bloomed everywhere, and it felt as if she'd reached out to remind us she loved us.

"Hey, Aunt Barb." Cramer met me at my car and helped with the unloading. Though they're all decent men, Cramer is my favorite nephew. If I had a son, I imagine he'd be a lot like Cramer, introspective, capable, and intuitive about people—except in the case of his wife/not wife/wife. Loyalty is a wonderful thing—except when it's not.

"How are you settling in out here?" I asked as we worked.

"I like it," he said. "Trees don't play loud music, and the animals are grateful for everything they get."

I waved toward the bunkhouse. "What can we get you to make that old place comfortable?"

He grinned. "I've got everything I need. Let me show you."

Faye and Retta had taken control of the meal, so I followed Cramer to the bunkhouse, which was vastly different from the musty, dusty shack I recalled. He'd installed fluorescent fixtures in two tracks down the entire ceiling, lighting the room with an efficient if not particularly warm glow. More than half of the long, low room was full of computer equipment. In the remaining section was an apartment-sized stove, a dormitory-type refrigerator, a microwave, a queen-sized bed, and a flat-screen TV the size of Rhode Island. The bunkhouse, once meant for many men, had become Cramer's place for many electronics.

Lunch was pleasant, and the girls chatted about gardening and animal care like old farm wives at a grange meeting. There were sad moments when they thought about their mom, but I knew they'd have such times on and off for a long time to come.

I was sure disaster would strike when Retta insisted Styx was going with us to the cabin. Faye's dog and Retta's dog hate each other—well, that's not true. Faye's dog hates Retta's dog, but he hates almost everyone. Styx doesn't hate anyone, but he knows he's not welcome in Buddy's world. It confuses his pea-sized brain, and he keeps trying and getting snapped at.

Apparently the farm served as a demilitarized zone. While Buddy didn't warm to Styx, he didn't object to his presence. And while Styx did his usual prancing-and-dancing moves, he gave Buddy space, tacitly admitting they'd never be besties.

We started walking, Styx exploring in wide circles around us and Buddy remaining at Faye's heels. Daisy had recovered her usual good spirits, and she pointed out objects along the way, pretty stones, cow-pies, and an occasional flowering weed that for some reason interested her more than dozens of others we passed.

When we got to the woods, Buddy stopped, growling low in his throat. Styx sniffed the air tentatively, too, as if he detected something new.

"What is it, boy?" The dog didn't answer Faye. What a surprise.

"Probably a deer," I said. "They must love it here with the planted fields all around and the trees for cover." Something I'd read came to mind and I said, "Did you know deer secrete a strong pheromone from a gland near their eyes?"

"How you doing, Daisy?" Retta asked. "Are you tired of walking?"

"I'm okay," the child replied. "I like it out here."

Another growl from Buddy. We stopped and listened, but we heard nothing. Just to be safe, I searched out a stout tree branch. If I didn't need it for protection, I could use it as a walking stick.

"Probably a deer, like you said," Faye remarked, and we went on.

"Yes. The article said antlers are the fastest-growing living tissue in the world. And deer can move their ears without moving their heads. Their eyes allow them—"

"Speaking of hearing," Retta interrupted, "Faye tells me you found a bug in your office."

"We did."

"So Gabe didn't alert them to our investigation. They were listening in all along."

"I'm sure Gabe visit to Farrell's store didn't help," I said.

Retta made an impatient sound with her lips. "I don't see how it could have hurt."

As we came up the last rise before the cabin, Buddy started barking, the hair on his neck bristling with tension. Not one to be left out, Styx added his deeper bark to Buddy's, making enough noise to wake the dead.

Pulling Daisy close, Faye crouched behind a tree. Retta and I chose our own trees, and we peered cautiously down the slope before us. The cabin looked much the same as before. For a split second I thought I saw movement on the other side of the pond, but as I turned to focus on it, there was nothing. It had been brown, a bird or a squirrel, most likely. Still, past events had made me cautious, and I waited, scanning the area around us.

Faye ordered Buddy to be quiet, and he stopped barking. Styx doesn't take orders, but when Buddy stopped making noise, he did too. The scene before us went quiet.

"Stay with Daisy," I told Faye. I started down the slope, taking cover when possible. Hearing a sound behind me, I turned to see Retta following. She stooped to pick up a branch, and I recalled the damage she'd done to a bad guy with a similar weapon on our last adventure. Giving her an encouraging nod, I continued toward the cabin. It felt good to have her at my back. For all her faults, Retta isn't afraid to wade into danger when it's required.

There was nothing there. The cabin was as we'd left it—or rather, as the sheriff's men had left it. After we looked in the corners, checked to see that the bunker was empty, and looked out both windows, Retta went out and signaled to Faye, who started toward us. Buddy seemed no longer worried about whatever he'd seen before, and I concluded it probably had been an animal.

Inside the cabin Daisy went directly to the box where Miss Gladiolus lay. "I bet you missed me!" she told the doll as she gave her a big hug. Our mission accomplished, we had nothing else to do there, but we lingered, taking in our childhood retreat and the changes that had been made to it.

After exploring the cabin briefly, Styx went back outside. I saw him pass the windows, his nose to the ground. When I heard the splash of water, I groaned. Newfs can't resist diving into any pond, river or lake they encounter, and I knew we'd be returning to Allport with a damp, slimy dog in the back of Retta's car.

When Styx returned, his big frame darkening the doorway, he had something in his mouth. "What did you find, Baby?" Retta asked.

Styx never gives his prizes up willingly. It's entertaining to watch Retta try to play catch with him because he goes after an object willingly, brings it within a few feet of her, and then resists all her attempts to get it back. That's what he did now, holding onto what he'd found and backing away when Retta approached.

I was only mildly interested. With Styx, the prize might be a stick, a piece of bark, or a rock. I've seen him play with half-rotten apples, tossing them into the air and running them down as if they had legs and were trying to escape.

This time, however, it was something else.

"Barbara Ann." Retta's voice sounded odd, and I turned to see what she'd wrestled away from the dog.

Daisy turned from introducing Buddy to Miss Gladiolus. "That's Momma's!" she cried. "Styx, where did you get my momma's shoe?"

CHAPTER FORTY-SIX

Faye

When Daisy identified the item Styx had found as Rose Isley's shoe, I looked from Barb to Retta, seeing grave concern in their eyes. Tacitly we agreed we couldn't let Daisy know what we suspected was outside the cabin.

"Daisy," Retta said briskly. "You and Faye take your dolly and go back to the house. I'll bet Bill's got the ice cream ready."

The child looked doubtful. "What about Momma?"

"Barbara Ann and I will look for her, won't we Barbara?"

"Yes," Barb replied, her voice choked. "We'll find her if we can."

"Will you bring her to the house so she can have ice cream too?"

Barb bit her lip before answering. "We will, Sweetie. If we can."

I kept up a stream of patter as Daisy and I walked, to keep her from looking around as well as to distract myself from visions of what Styx might bring to Retta next. What would my sisters find out there? I guessed it wouldn't be pretty.

When we got near the house Daisy called, "Styx found Momma's shoe in the woods. Miz Evans and Retta are looking for her."

Pansy rose immediately. "I'll go help them." Iris looked to me and read the message in my eyes. "Stay here," she ordered. "They'll call Mrs. Burner if they find her. Then we'll all go."

As Carla dished up ice cream, I took Bill aside and told him what had happened. "What should we do?" he asked.

"I think I should take the girls home," I replied. "If Barb and Retta find Rose, there'll be police all over this place in half an hour."

He nodded, his gaze turning toward the three girls who sat in a little circle, eating homemade ice cream. "I'll let Carla know what's going on." He shook his head sadly. "They're such nice kids. You'll have to bring them back out in a day or two so they can ride the horses." His eyes said more: that the girls had something terrible to face, and he wanted to be able to help them get past it when they were ready.

"Yes," I said, my throat thick with sorrow. "Pansy will like that."

We made a quick plan. Bill went inside the house and called my phone. I pretended to speak to Barb then reported to the girls that they hadn't found anything. I said Barb reminded me we had paperwork that had to be filed by the end of the day, so we had to head back to town right away. When Daisy asked about the dogs, I said they were having a really good time in the woods, so Retta would bring them along later.

It was the most lying I've done in a long time, and it was only doable because I didn't want them to know their mother lay out in the woods somewhere, dead.

Iris didn't believe it for one second. Pansy was clearly reluctant to leave, but Iris spoke softly to her. Her face stiff with knowledge she shouldn't have to bear, Iris helped Daisy get into my car, buckling her in with the seatbelt.

It was two hours before Retta and Barb returned, looking exhausted. On his home turf, Buddy turned territorial and growled at Styx. Retta invited the girls to come with her as she took Styx out to Dale's workshop. While they were outside, Barb told me what they'd found.

"She was in the pond, out where the deep hole is. It's hard to tell with the decomposition, but they said her skull is damaged, consistent with a blow to the back of the head."

"So McAdams killed Rose and sank her body in the pond."

"He weighed it down with some bricks from that pile in the yard." She sighed. "It's hard to say if he hoped it was a permanent burial or if he intended to move the body later. He must have known the pond would shrink over the summer."

"We'll never know, I guess. Ben didn't expect to fall off that silo."

Barb paced a little. "He needed to hide her body until he used the weapon hidden in the bunker for whatever they're planning. After that, he probably intended to disappear."

"Or kill himself in his crazy plot," I said. "Either way, he didn't care what happened to the girls."

Barb smiled grimly. "They're girls. How much could they matter?"

Sheriff Brill pulled up out front a few minutes later, and I saw he'd stopped to get the psychologist, Julie Walters. I was surprised when Bill's Honda pulled up and he and Carla got out.

The four of them entered together, and I made introductions. Carla told the sheriff, "We came to support the girls."

Brill and Julie joined the girls in my living room. Barb, Retta, Carla, Bill, and I stayed in the kitchen, waiting. Dale came in and stood near the door, his eyes sad.

First the sheriff came out. "Julie will do what she can to help them cope. She's also going to arrange things with the school. When they're ready, the girls can finish this year so they can start in September in the right grade levels." He shook his head. "It'll give them something to concentrate on, Julie thinks. So they can begin to deal with their mom's death."

"I could help," Carla said. "I have a teaching degree."

Brill nodded. "I'll get out of your hair now. You people have been seeing way too much of me lately."

"And you've been wonderful." Retta patted his arm. "Let us know if you find out more about what those men were planning."

Assuring us he would, Brill left. We sat at the table, waiting for the girls and hoping they'd be able to handle their latest tragedy.

CHAPTER FORTY-SEVEN

Barb

Retta did a good job with the girls over the next few days. Faye and Carla went out to her house at some point each day, taking little treats and gifts. I only went once. It was hard for me to witness Pansy's sadness, and though I thought she liked me, she retreated from everyone except her sisters.

I understood. There are griefs that can't be spoken, that are somehow trivialized by talking to strangers about them. That's how I see loss, and I suspected Pansy felt the same way.

The cat was coming to my window pretty regularly, trusting I'd have food for her. She still didn't want to be petted, but if I set my hand on the windowsill, she'd nudge it the way cats do in order to transfer their scent to you.

I toyed with the idea of capturing the cat as a gift for Pansy. It might make her feel better, since I hadn't yet seen an animal she didn't connect with. On the other hand, Pansy's future was undetermined. She might not be allowed a cat at her new home. I decided next time she was at the house I'd bring her upstairs and introduce her to my cat. It might help a little.

It didn't take long for the authorities to complete Rose's autopsy and release her body. Rory reported she died from a blow to the back of her head. Searching the house, they'd found blood on one of the kitchen cabinet doors. "They think the door was open, probably because Rose was putting away dishes," Rory said. "They argued and Ben struck her, causing her to stumble back and hit her head on the corner of the door. She died almost instantly."

"Are they sure Ben did it?"

"They're sure he dumped her body into the pond."

"I wonder if she asked one too many questions about what he was doing down in that cabin," I murmured.

"Possible," Rory agreed. "Ben was a tense guy, and if he was planning to use that grenade launcher for some big event, he was likely more stressed than usual." He sighed. "Anyway, there's no sign anyone was in the kitchen except Ben, Rose, and the girls." He grinned. "That's assuming we eliminate Faye, Dale, Carla, and Bill from the list of possible suspects."

With the verdict that a domestic dispute had turned tragic, we were allowed to bury Rose four days after she was found. We looked forward to the funeral, hoping when it was over, the girls could begin to recover.

The question of what would happen to them afterward was unsettled. Despite our fondness, none of us was prepared to take on three children. Faye fussed about it but had to admit we were all past the desire to take on parental duties 24/7.

We included the girls in the funeral arrangements, feeling it would help if they were part of things. I was prepared to pay, but Sheriff Brill called to tell us Rose had a small life insurance policy that would cover a simple funeral. I added a few extras I thought the girls would appreciate and, with some reluctance, asked Cronk to officiate. While he wasn't my idea of a shining pastoral example, the girls were used to him, even seemed to like him.

We entered the church in a clump, aware of the stares of the curious. I'd paid for the girls' funeral outfits, though Retta had insisted on doing the shopping. I was proud of the way they held their heads up. Funerals test a person's mettle, and when I must attend one, I prefer to do so with a dignified mien.

The little church was full. The whole regular congregation was there to support the girls. After we were seated and before the pastor started, Colt Farrell entered, head up like the lord of the manor and took the last chair in the front row. His wife Joan was in the kitchen, Retta whispered, readying treats for afterward.

I turned, pretending to search for someone, and took stock of the men present. One of them resembled the picture we'd found online of Floyd Stone. When I turned back, Pansy met my eyes and nodded assent. "Grave Stone," Daisy had called him. He certainly looked grave.

Since Pansy had noticed what I was doing, I mouthed a question: Sharky? She looked around again, hiding her search with an expression of casual interest. A few seconds later she met my gaze again and shook her head. He wasn't there.

After the service, we stayed for the sake of politeness, chatting with members of the congregation who came to express their condolences. Retta was unrepentant about her earlier charade, and I noticed Joan Farrell shooting metaphorical daggers at her with her eyes. A woman she introduced as Dee gave each of the girls a hug, telling them to call her if they ever needed anything. A couple of the men made attempts to be supportive, and I admitted to myself this was a group of well-meaning, kind people for the most part. Only Farrell and Stone stood in a corner, pointedly avoiding us.

With a burst of decision, I approached them. "It seems things turned out badly for your friend."

"Rose's death was an unfortunate accident." Farrell spoke to Stone, barely glancing at me.

"A good person doesn't hide an accident, Mr. Farrell."

He sniffed. "The girls hid Ben's body to hide their sin, just as Ben hid Rose's body to hide his."

"They're children. They were afraid. What's Ben's excuse?"

Again Farrell spoke more to Stone than to me. "Maybe he had things he needed to get done."

I felt my face burn as anger shook me. "Did you know McAdams killed Rose? Did you leave the girls out there with that monster?"

The look I got was full of contempt. "Miss Evans, it might surprise you to know that men—unlike you women—can keep a secret. They don't run to their friends and confess everything." He raised a hand. "Ben kept his secrets to himself. I respect that, though I cannot condone what he did. None of us are perfect."

None of us *IS* perfect! I wanted to say. The pronoun *none* is singular. But it was a funeral. In a church. Not an occasion for a Correction Event.

When cookies had been eaten, condolences offered, and most of the people were gone, I escorted the girls to Retta's car. "I'll pick you up tomorrow around 11:00," I told them. "You're going to meet a foreign dignitary."

"What's a digunterry?" Daisy asked.

"You'll see tomorrow," Retta told her. "Right now, I think we should go back to my house, change our clothes, and take Styx for a long, long walk along the riverbank."

Faye and I stayed at the church, having a secondary task to accomplish. Ben McAdams' body awaited burial, but we hadn't mentioned that to the girls. Retta had suggested we might use the deposit money Ben had paid when he moved in to cover a simple cremation. We intended to ask Cronk to handle it, since we felt no further obligation to Ben McAdams.

Faye began by thanking Cronk for the moving tribute he'd given Rose. When he bowed gravely, hands crossed at his waist in a pious stance, I brought up the subject of McAdams' burial.

"I believe Ben was at heart a good man," Cronk said as his cheeks flopped. "He made one tragic mistake and followed it with a second, but he was a man of Bible principles. I'll be honored to send him to the Lord."

"The Lord might not want him," I muttered.

I doubt Cronk heard the words, but he caught my tone. "Miss, all of us are welcome in the Kingdom if we admit our sins." As if he couldn't stop himself, he added, "And pride is a terrible sin."

"So is killing someone and hiding her body."

His lips clamped closed, and I told myself it would do no good to antagonize the man. Faye stepped in to smooth things over. "Pastor, we'll very much appreciate you taking responsibility for the service." She explained about the deposit we intended to use for Ben's final expenses.

It was better than Ben deserved, in my opinion, but I saw a way to turn Cronk's cooperation to our advantage. "It will give your congregation a chance to say goodbye. Surely there are some people who liked Ben, even if he was a misogynistic murderer." After a pause I asked, "Who would that be, Mr. Cronk? Who were McAdams' closest friends?"

The pastor held his pious pose, but his eyes flashed with anger. "I doubt anyone could say he was Ben's close friend, Ms. Evans."

Beside me Faye's fingers flexed spasmodically. She was dying for a cigarette. Though she doesn't smoke much anymore, when Faye needs her fix, she needs it.

"All right, who thought the way McAdams did? Who in your congregation agreed with his views on women?"

Cronk hesitated before answering. "This church preaches values we take directly from the Bible."

"Yes," Faye shot me a look that warned me to keep quiet.

"One of those values is the family. The husband is the head, the wife supports him, and the children are the future generation."

I wanted to argue, but Faye shot me a look, so I didn't.

"Everyone here accepts that?"

He smiled grimly. "To a degree. People like Dee Johnson are on one end of the spectrum. They accept male leadership but contend women should still have a voice."

"And Ben McAdams was on the opposite end?"

He sighed. "Yes."

I'd have bet that only men who shared Ben's prejudices deserved any consideration from his God, and probably white Anglo-Saxon Protestant men at that. "Thank you for officiating, Mr. Cronk. My sister and I will let you get back to your flock." I wanted to add "of sheep," but I restrained myself.

CHAPTER FORTY-EIGHT

Retta

When I pulled into the driveway, there was a pickup truck that looked vaguely familiar. As the occupants got out, I realized Gabe was the driver. On the other side was a pretty girl so tiny she appeared at first to be a child. It was only when I looked closely that I saw she was in her twenties with dark brown hair, green eyes, and a delicate face.

"Hi, Mrs. Stilson," Gabe said. "This is Mindy. We wanted to come to the funeral, but Mindy just got off work."

Mindy had brought a small gift for each girl, hair bands she'd crocheted and decorated. She expressed her condolences in a piping voice that matched her youthful appearance. Iris, who was an inch or so taller than Mindy, thanked her for her concern.

Delaying our walk, we invited them to sit on the patio. I introduced the girls then went inside to get drinks for everyone. When I came back out, Mindy had the girls talking about some singer they all apparently liked. She had the interpersonal skills to be a good social worker, for she listened as each girl spoke and responded in a way that let them know they were taken seriously.

Gabe sat watching her, his face shining with affection. It was hard to see what Mindy saw in him. She was nearing a college degree, dressed fashionably, and presented herself well. Gabe was recently out of jail, a high school dropout who spoke like he'd skipped most of his English classes. That's often the way with people, though. Gabe has a good heart, and maybe that's exactly what Mindy was looking for.

As we talked, I remembered something Faye had mentioned. "I understand you're going to attend a conference soon."

"Yes," Mindy replied. "A few of us who've shown leadership at the college were asked to attend." She twisted her hands. "I'm a little nervous, because we're going to be introduced as WALL's Leaders of Tomorrow, and we each have to say a few words."

"You can handle that," I assured her. "When will this be?"

"Less than a week now," she said. "We're going to—"

At that moment, my dog decided he wasn't getting enough attention. Bounding up to the table, Styx knocked it sideways with his big old body. All the drinks went toppling over, and Mindy's iced tea landed directly in her lap.

She was really nice about it, but that was the end of the visit. Walking stiffly because of her wet pants, Mindy told us goodbye, and Gabe took her home to get dry clothes.

CHAPTER FORTY-NINE

Barb

The day after Rose's funeral was the occasion of President Bahn's visit. We'd had a serious discussion about whether to take the Isley girls along. As an alumna, Retta was involved in the planning, and she thought they should attend. "How often will they get to see a head of state, and a female at that?" she asked. "They can even meet her."

"Somebody's out there with a grenade launcher," Faye argued. "No matter how many cops are there, it could be dangerous."

In the end I sided with Retta. While I recognized the danger, I was confident our police could prevent it.

President Bahn made a gracious speech, refreshments were served, and we all continued on our way without incident. Anyone paying attention would have noticed a considerable police presence in addition to the president's own security. Rory had most of his people on duty, as did the sheriff. State police officers stood guard, and several men and women with ear buds, probably federal agents, scanned the crowd with no-nonsense scrutiny.

Retta finagled an introduction for the six of us. We got no more than a gracious nod and a murmur of acknowledgement from the president, but the girls were awed by the experience, stiff with tension at the moment they faced the lady, and overcome with giggles once we were away.

Faye took the girls to our house, Retta stayed to help with the clean-up, and Rory and I unwound a little by taking a drive along the shore of Lake Huron. Being near the water is a calming influence for me. In Tacoma, when things at the D.A.'s office got really difficult, I'd often gone somewhere to watch marine animals play or listen to the water slap against the shoreline. When life gets tough, it helps to remind yourself of the enormity of the world and the transitory nature of one person's problems.

As we drove southward, racing an ore-boat headed the same direction, we spoke of the danger that hadn't come to pass. Rory told me what those up the chain of authority had shared with him. "There's no evidence linking Farrell or Stone to the stolen weapon. They admit to meeting Sharky twice at Ben's, but as far as they knew, he was there only to play cards."

"Do you think the plan was all Ben and Sharky's doing?"

Rory scratched absently at a mosquito bite on his arm. "Honestly? No. The bug in your office has to be Farrell's work. He was caught on your farm twice, clearly looking for the weapon."

"And Stone?"

"From what Faye said, he seems likely to be part of it."

"So there were four of them. When Ben died in the fall, it was a problem to continue but not an impossibility."

"But now Sharky's taken off, and their secret is out," Rory said. "They still have the weapon, but without their sharpshooter and the element of surprise, they knew they were likely to fail."

"Sharky missing, Ben dead," I said. "Easy for the other two to walk away and let the blame fall on them."

"Farrell admitted to the feds that Sharky was kind of creepy."

"If full-grown adults get that feeling from him, it's easy to see why the girls did. "There's no word about where he might have gone?"

"It appears Ben taught Sharky some of his tricks for going off the grid. Sharky hasn't had a job since the nursing home fired him. He rented his house, and we found his car sitting behind it. He might be on a train bound for California, or he might be living in somebody's garage in the middle of Allport. We just don't know."

As Rory spoke, the cabin came to mind. Sharky knew it was there, knew it was stocked with supplies. "Are you working tomorrow?"

He grinned. "Is this your way of asking me for a date?"

"Not exactly. We're going to the farm to see if Sharky's hiding out in the cabin down by the pond."

CHAPTER FIFTY

Faye

I almost let the phone go to voicemail, since the readout showed a number unknown to me. I try not to answer when I don't recognize the source, but there's always a nagging fear I'll miss something important. On the chance it wasn't a robot trolling for responses, I answered.

"Is this Faye Burner?" The man's voice sounded strained, like someone who didn't enjoy talking on the phone.

"Yes."

"Walt Dunham here. I live in the U.P. near Hessel, on Second Home Farm."

"Oh! Yes, Mr. Dunham. I wrote to you."

"That's why I'm calling. You said you'd like an old horse."

"Well, not me. My sons have taken over the family farm, and we're exploring the idea of retiring draft horses there."

"Well, I have a situation up here. A guy up on Mackinac Island called, and he has a horse that needs a place right away. He thought he'd get one more summer out of her, but it don't look like that's going to happen. She can't pull, and he says her breathing ain't right."

"Oh, the poor thing!"

Dunham didn't waste time echoing my dismay. "He wants me to take her, but my wife and I are trying to work our way out of the business. We're getting old, and she wants to go to Florida in the winters. I'm not taking any more horses, and we're trying to relocate the ones we've got now."

As the purpose of Dunham's call hit, I felt alternating waves of joy and anxiety. "You want us to take this horse for you?"

"Well, you'd be dealing with the owner. I just told him I'd contact you and see if you're still interested."

Clearing my throat, I said it. "Yes, we are. We have the space, and I spoke with a local veterinarian about care. She'll donate her time if we pay for medicines and supplies."

"Sounds like you're going at it the right way," Dunham said. "There's another problem, though. The owner's gearing up for the tourist season, and he's crazy busy. He says he'll split the expense if you can go there and take the horse off his hands."

Though I hadn't thought about going to Mackinac Island myself to get a horse, I had considered transport for them. The farmer who leases our fields, Chet Masters, owns a horse trailer, and he offered me the use of it a few days earlier in exchange for letting his daughter's Arabian stay with my two on the farm.

"She had to have a horse," Chet told me. "Then two years later she discovered boys. She doesn't want her pet sold, but she doesn't spend near the time riding she used to. The poor old thing is all alone over here. If you'll keep her with yours, you can use my trailer as you need to. I'll help out with feed too."

"I can arrange to pick up the horse." I told Dunham.

Walt gave me a phone number, and after two attempts, I reached a harassed-sounding man who admitted to being the owner of a twelve-year-old horse named Dolly. "She's not deathly sick or anything," he said, "but there's something wrong with her lungs. Honestly, ma'am, I don't have time to nurse her, and the tourists don't like seeing sick animals. I don't want the ASPCA or whoever up here hassling me, so the sooner she's gone, the better."

"I'm willing," I said, "but how do I get her across the straits?"

"There's a retired vet in Cheboygan who'll bring her across and help load her into your trailer. I can call him and set it up."

He made it sound as if he was doing me a favor rather than vice versa, but I didn't care. There was a horse who needed me. My heart felt full. We had our first retired horse, and I intended to make her last days on earth peaceful and filled with love.

CHAPTER FIFTY-ONE

Barb

Bill and Carla were coming out the drive when Rory and I turned in and met them halfway. They stopped and got out to greet us, and I told them Rory and I planned to walk to the cabin.

"Why would he be out there?" Bill asked.

"He knows it's out there and stocked with food," I replied. "He knows the police want to talk to him, and he might think they won't find him out there."

"We're supposed to meet our lawyer early tomorrow morning," Bill said. "We planned to spend the night with friends in Traverse City, but we can change it around if you need us."

"We're just going to check to see if anyone's back there. It's unlikely he's there, so you two go ahead and do as you planned."

Carla got into the car, but Bill hesitated. "Have you heard from Mom? She's apparently lined up our first retired draft horse."

"She found a horse?"

"I think it found her," Bill said with a chuckle. "She said she might go today when Cramer gets off work, but it'll be tomorrow at the latest. Apparently the animal's pretty sick, and the owner doesn't want the tourists to see it and assume it isn't being tended."

I wondered briefly how Faye and her sons would deal with the probability the horses they took in didn't have long to live.

With one foot inside the car, Bill repeated his offer. "Maybe we should call and reschedule things."

"No, really," I told him. "If by some chance Sharky's out there, we'll call the sheriff in."

Bill seemed torn until Rory repeated what I'd said, almost word for word. Nodding as if he finally understood, Bill got into the car and put it into gear. I glanced at Rory, who gave me a sheepish grin. Men hearing things from other men makes all the difference.

We watched Bill and Carla until they turned onto the road, their vehicle ticking like Captain Hook's crocodile, then proceeded to the barnyard gate.

Rory and I walked up the hill together, entered the woods, and followed the path. As we approached the cabin, we stopped talking and watched where our feet fell. If by some chance Sharky was hiding out there, we didn't want to broadcast our coming.

The cabin was quiet but not peaceful. We'd padlocked the door, but someone had torn it from its hinges. It hung crookedly to one side, pocked with sharp indentations, and

I pictured Sharky beating it in with something, a tire iron, maybe. I felt a hitch of dread between my shoulders.

Rory stopped me with an outstretched hand. "Go back to the house," he said softly. "As soon as you're out of hearing, call Sheriff Brill and tell him to send at least four men. Wait for them and guide them out here. I'll make sure he stays put."

I opened my mouth to argue, but Rory turned slightly to show me the gun holstered at the back of his jeans. Trust a cop to be prepared. Squeezing his arm, I turned and hurried off.

When I was far enough away, I took my phone from my pocket and made the call. By the time I cleared the woods, I had Brill's assurance he'd be there as soon as possible.

For half an hour I stood at the barnyard gate with nothing to do but listen to the silence. Pacing back and forth along the fence, I awaited the cavalry, disturbing the reindeer who followed my course, sniffing to see if I had anything to eat in my pockets.

The sheriff's arrival took longer than I thought I could stand. At one end of my path I peered down the driveway to see if they were coming. At the other end, I craned my neck to see if there was anyone up by the barn. I listened for gunshots. I plotted what I would do if Sharky came running down the hill. By the time I finally heard a car turn in from the road and saw the sheriff's brown cruiser coming toward me, I was nearly a wreck.

"Where is he?" Brill asked as he got out. A second cruiser pulled up behind him, lights flashing, and two young men in uniform got out. A few seconds later, a third car joined the others.

"It's about a half mile back." I pointed toward the woods.

Unsnapping his holster, Brill gestured in the direction I'd indicated. "Lead the way."

With the sheriff and his deputies close behind, I retraced my path. We said little and spoke only in low tones, tensed and ready.

Our stealthy approach was unnecessary. We arrived at the cabin to find Rory standing in the doorway, his face grim. "He's in there," he told us, "but it's too late. He's dead."

CHAPTER FIFTY-TWO

When a call came from an unknown source, I again debated letting it ring. I had a lot to do, but Retta had begun taking over the planning. Barb gets irritated when she does that, but I don't mind. Retta's very organized, and if a person's willing to give up a little autonomy, she gets things done.

It was the office phone, though, so I felt compelled to answer. "Smart Detective Agency."

"It's Pastor Cronk at River Church."

"Hello, Pastor. Faye Burner here. What can we do for you?"

"I'm hoping it's the other way around. Ms. Evans asked who Ben McAdams counted as friends, and I should have been more forthcoming." He chuckled. "Your sister's a formidable woman."

I had to smile in response. "I think you've found the perfect word."

"She ruffled my feathers a little, I'll admit. I'm afraid she colors all of our congregation with the same brush."

263

"Barb doesn't tolerate inequality very well."
Remembering my loyalties I added, "I don't much
appreciate it either."

"I won't lecture you on Scripture," Cronk said, "but
after you left I prayed about my response. I answered your
sister's animosity with my own, which was a prideful
mistake. I know things I should have told you."

"What things?"

He sighed. "After Ben and Rose moved in together, I
went out there quite often, feeling it was my duty to see
them married. The world no longer requires it, but in our
congregation, folks are encouraged to get their lives right
with God."

"Rose refused to marry Ben."

"She did. In time I understood why. Ben was a good
man in many ways, but he had blind spots. One of them
was a friend of his, Richard Stark."

"You met Sharky?"

"Only once, but I saw immediately that Rose didn't
like him. She tensed up whenever he came near her or one
of her daughters."

"And what was your impression?"

Cronk's hesitation told me more than an answer would
have. Finally he said, "I think he has a disturbed soul. I
invited him to come to services at the church, but he
seemed to think that was a joke."

"Did Stark know any other men in your
congregation?"

"Again, my conscience troubles me, but I feel I must be completely honest. I once heard Ben mention Floyd Stone to Mr. Stark. It was obvious they both knew him, because they joked about his size."

"How well do you know Stone?"

He cleared his throat before answering. "He's pretty quiet. Mostly he throws in an 'Amen!' when Colt speaks about women in the church."

"Ten steps behind the menfolk, I guess."

"Mrs. Burner, ours is a Bible-teaching church. We read and study the Scriptures and try to do as they instruct. I don't want to imply that I disagree with Mr. Farrell completely, it's just that—Well, to be honest, I'd find it hard to do what I do without the women of the church. If they can't lead, we'll have no choir, no Sunday school, and no one to do mission work. All of those groups are run by dedicated women."

"So women can lead as long as it's in service to the church."

"Exactly. I'm very grateful for their help, so you can see it's difficult for me to walk the line between the two sides. I know what the Bible says, but I suppose there were women in the background during our Lord's ministry, seeing that things got done."

Women in the background. I sighed. I wasn't likely to convince Cronk that a woman's brain was of as much value as his own or Colt Farrell's. "Is there anything else you recall that might help us?"

"Nothing more. I'd help if I could."

"We appreciate that, Pastor. Please call if you remember anything more."

I called Barb to pass on Cronk's information, but she didn't answer. Knowing Rory was with her, I phoned him. He sounded tense, and I guessed they were in the middle of something. "Sorry to bother you, but I knew you'd want to hear this." I related Cronk's information, ending with, "You might talk to him yourself. I probably didn't ask the right things."

"You did fine, Faye," Rory replied. "You're the type people open up to."

I chuckled. "Yeah, every cashier in every discount store in the world opens up to me: 'I haven't had a break in seven hours,' 'My son just called to tell me his girlfriend is pregnant' 'My back is killing me.'" I got back to my purpose. "Will you pass the information on to Barb?"

"I will," he said, "but she's with Sheriff Brill right now. We found Sharky's body in your cabin, they're discussing how she guessed where to look."

"Sharky's body?" I asked, horrified. "What happened to him?"

"It looks like suicide."

"Looks like?"

I could almost see his shrug. "He was shot through the head, but I try not to jump to conclusions."

"What does Barb think?"

"We haven't had a chance to talk about it. Brill thinks Stark killed himself when the plot to assassinate Madame Bahn fell apart."

His phrasing caught my attention. "What do you think?"

Rory sighed. "I'd be a lot more relaxed if we'd found the grenade launcher in the cabin with Stark's body."

"Maybe he hid it."

"They've got men with metal detectors looking all over the farm. If it's here, they'll find it."

CHAPTER FIFTY-THREE

Retta

The girls and I helped with cleanup after Madame Bahn's speech, stacking chairs and picking up litter. On the way home we stopped at the grocery store for a few items. I got a kick out of seeing them choose what to buy. Iris read every label before deciding, Pansy wanted to try it all, and Daisy liked anything that came in a brightly-colored package. It was almost 3:00 when we reached home. As we unloaded my cloth shopping bags, Faye called to say she intended to head to Mackinac Island to pick up a horse.

"Who's going with you?"

"Cramer said he'd leave work early. Bill and Carla are away until tomorrow night, but there's a guy who'll help Cramer and me get the horse across the Straits and into Chet's trailer."

"You and Cramer are going to bring a two thousand pound animal all that way by yourselves?"

"Sure." She tried to sound brave, but I knew she must be scared half to death. Cramer knew even less than Faye did about horses. What kind of helper would he be?

"Faye Darlene," I told her, "here's what you're going to do. You're going to call that man back and tell him you'll come for the horse tomorrow. Have Cramer take the whole day off. I'll follow you up there in case something goes wrong."

"What about the girls?"

"They can come along. I'll bet they've never been there, so while you're making arrangements, I can show them the sights."

Faye didn't argue. It's one of the things I like most about her.

An hour later, Barbara Ann called with a different kind of news. "Sharky is dead?" I repeated when she told me.

"Apparently he killed himself. From what people say, he was pretty unstable."

"When the plan to kill Madame Bahn failed, he gave up?"

"Faye seems to think that's likely."

Of course she'd called Faye first.

"What do you think about Faye taking on another horse?"

"I think if she doesn't do what she's always wanted to do at her age, she's likely never going to get to do it."

"So the fact she plans to bring a sick horse all this way with just Cramer for help makes sense to you?"

"Cramer's more capable than you think," Barbara replied. "He's just not one to jump up and take control."

"That's putting it mildly." I outlined my idea for a trip. "Someone should be there in case the truck breaks down or something."

"Why? Because Faye doesn't have a cell phone and doesn't know how to call for help?"

"You don't have to be sarcastic, Barbara. I'm going for moral support." An idea struck. "You should come along. We can show the girls the island, maybe have tea on the porch of the Grand Hotel. Wouldn't that be a treat for them?"

"I can't remember the last time I was on Mackinac Island."

"It's very educational," I said, guessing that would sway her. "All that history. And Pansy will love the horses."

"I suppose we could make a day of it. The girls certainly deserve some fun, and so do we after this last week."

CHAPTER FIFTY-FOUR

Barb

Retta probably thought she was really clever to have talked me into a trip to Mackinac Island, but I meant what I said about all of us deserving a break. Faye, Retta, and I had been through a lot in the last few days. The Isley girls' lives would never be the same. A day on the island is like a little escape from the world. It couldn't restore their former happiness, but it couldn't hurt.

What I needed at the moment was a Correction Event. I felt the urge to set something right, and I'd happened on an error very close to home that would be simple and satisfying to fix. At the corner of my block, a local artist had put up a sign to indicate she had handmade goods for sale. I'd heard she was quite talented, but sadly, she wasn't grammatically aware. Her sign advertised ART'S & CRAFT'S, as if her arts and crafts owned something.

I'd seen the sign on my morning walk, noting its white background. The mistakes could be easily corrected with two small squares of white duct tape. I'd stop, ostensibly with some minor irritation like a pebble in my shoe. If no one was looking, I'd slap the tape over the offending apostrophes and be on my way.

There's a saying that in theory, a practice should be easy, but in practice it seldom is. I should have waited until the next morning, but with the trip to Mackinac scheduled, I knew I wouldn't have time to get my walk in. The day after the trip was a possibility, but I was eager to see those apostrophes gone. I should have waited. The chances of discovery are much less at 6:00 a.m.

At first it was as easy as I'd imagined. I took off my shoe, leaning on the sign as if for support. The squares of duct tape were inside my shirt, and I quickly peeled one then the other off, covering the offending apostrophes. To a casual observer it appeared I had to move my hand to keep my balance, and that was perfect.

What wasn't perfect was the voice I heard when I put my shoe back on. "What did you just do?"

Retta had stopped her car in the middle of the street, and her expression betrayed surprise and a glint of humor. I berated myself. If I'd done this on my walk, she'd never have caught me. Retta seldom leaves her bed before 8:00 a.m.

I shushed her, approaching the car so we could speak in low tones. "Nothing," I said, but she didn't believe me for a second.

"You changed that sign, didn't you, Barbara Ann?"

I sighed, resigning myself to what was coming. "It was incorrect."

Conclusions were reached behind her eyes. "You're the one who's been fixing spelling errors around town. People have noticed."

I looked around nervously. "Do we have to do this in the street?"

"No." She was still smiling. "Let's go into the house."

She parked her car out front. I waited for her to get out then led the way inside, glancing nervously around to see who might be watching. "Where are the girls?"

"There's a puppet show at the library. I came over to make sure we're ready for the trip tomorrow." She gestured toward the sign, humor dancing in her eyes. "And what do I find!"

She sat down at the kitchen table. I delayed, offering iced tea and some of Faye's famous peanut butter cookies. Retta accepted both, but her sly look let me know I wouldn't get off easily.

"I should have known it was you." She took a dainty bite.

Honestly seemed best. "Retta, I can't eliminate child abuse or war or corruption in our government. For decades I worked for justice, but the world is still wrong in a lot of ways." I paused, and for once Retta didn't comment. She merely waited for me to go on. "Grammatical mistakes are different. You find something that's wrong; you fix it, and it's right."

"You do that. Not most people." She sipped her tea. "In fact, nobody I know of—at least until now."

I shrugged. "Errors bother me."

She was silent for a few seconds. "Know what bothers me?"

I didn't answer, because I was going to hear it anyway.

"It bothers me to be an auxiliary investigator in my sisters' detective agency. It bothers me to get called in only when you need my social and business contacts. I have a brain, you know."

"Retta—"

"So here's the deal." She met my gaze, letting me know she was serious. "I know about your—" She stopped, unable to think of a term for what I do.

"Correction Events."

She smiled, amused that I had a proper title for my improper actions. "—your correction events. If I were caught at something like that, I'd laugh it off, but I know you. You don't want anybody, not Faye and especially not Rory, to know about it, am I right?"

I nodded.

She shrugged lightly. "Well, I'm willing to keep your secret."

A rush of gratitude hit, followed by a sense of dread. With Retta there's always a trade-off. Being the youngest, she learned early to negotiate, and she's ruthless about getting what she wants.

Retta raised her hand as if swearing an oath. "If I become a full member of the Smart Detective Agency, I will never tell anyone about your Correction Events." Now her hands made quotation marks in the air. "Ever."

There it was. How much did I want Retta excluded? How much was I willing to give up to keep my secret?

It didn't take me long to make the decision, since there were only unfortunate options. "Agreed."

"Great!" In a remarkably humble tone for Retta she added, "I promise I'll try not to take over or boss you around."

I appreciated Retta's admission that she might do that, even if it was a promise she could never keep. It was like me promising to join the Allport Follies and dress as a clown. "Thank you."

"And I actually appreciate what you do."

"You mean creeping around nights like an aging Batgirl?"

She chuckled and took another bite of cookie. "You're not the only one who notices all those errors out there, Barbara Ann."

CHAPTER FIFTY-FIVE

Cramer had the trailer hitched to his truck when I got to the farm the next morning, and soon we were driving north. "Bill called from Traverse City last night," he told me, driving with practiced ease. "He says Carla really likes the Isley girls."

Something in Cramer's voice said there was more. "And?"

"Well, we got to talking about it. The farm's what they know, and the house is certainly big enough for more than Bill and Carla, so we wondered if they could stay out there."

"You want to take the girls in?"

"Well, not me. Bill and Carla would petition to become foster parents." He frowned. "The girls might not want to come."

"Oh, I think they would, but Bill and Carola don't know them very well."

He adjusted his side mirror slightly then rolled the window back up. "From what I've seen of the system, foster parents usually don't. You take in a child, or children in this case, and you make it work if you can. Carla's a great role model, and Bill and I could learn a lot from them about taking care of the animals." He added, "They got a bad deal. We'd like to give them a better one."

My heart swelled in my chest at evidence that my sons are good men. Not rich, not socially or physically impressive. Good men. That's enough for me.

We met Doc Hopkins, the vet who'd agreed to help with the horse, at a restaurant, where we bought him breakfast. Hopkins brought to mind a banty rooster Dad once had on the farm. Small, energetic, and unlikely to defer to anyone, Hopkins greeted me and Cramer with brisk friendliness. "Bought you a horse farm, eh?" he said as we shook hands. "You don't look crazy."

I explained about the renters who'd left us with a mix of animals, ending with, "I've always wanted to keep horses, and Cramer and Bill, my other son, agreed to give it a chance."

"Hope they've thought it through," the doc said. "Animals tie a person down. If you've got two or three people working together, though, it might be okay." He took off his cap, rubbed his bald head, and set it back in place. "If there's anything I can do to help out, call. I don't practice anymore, but that doesn't mean I gave up caring for critters."

"We'll be grateful if you get this horse across the straits for us."

"Won't be a problem as long as she can stand up." The waitress set a plate piled with pancakes before him, and he reached for the syrup. "What else you got on this farm?"

I listed the animals, and Hopkins lifted a brow. "Reindeer, eh? Do you plan to breed them?"

"Yes," Cramer replied. "Pansy says they lost a couple, though. Last year one was born dead and another only lived a few days."

"Soil around here lacks selenium," Hopkins said. "That can cause failure to conceive and calves that don't thrive. You need to supplement their diet with selenium salt blocks."

Cramer took out a pen, and I handed him a scrap of paper from my purse. "Selenium," he said, writing it down.

The two men talked as we ate, and I mostly listened. Cramer told Hopkins things he'd noticed, and the vet gave advice.

When the plates were empty, Hopkins piled his silverware and trash on his and leaned his elbows on the table. "Sounds like you had an interesting time the last few days."

Cramer smiled, catching my eye. The vet didn't know the half of it.

Hopkins slapped the table in a gesture of readiness. "Let's get your horse back here and into the truck so you can start getting acquainted."

CHAPTER FIFTY-SIX

Barb

I almost changed my mind as Faye bustled around getting ready the next morning. What seemed like an adventure at first now shifted to a trial with crowds of people, cold winds off the Straits, the smell of horse manure, and Retta's chirpy chatter. Only the thought of seeing Pansy having a good time made me stick to my decision to go.

"They're very excited," Retta had said during her third call to finalize our (her) plans. "Iris is dignified about it, not out of control like Pansy, who keeps jumping around the kitchen singing some song about being crazy over horses. Daisy doesn't really know what Mackinac Island is, but Pansy's got her acting silly too."

In my head, I defended the girl's actions as perfectly normal for a nine-year-old. Iris was a more sedate child, to be sure. It would be nice if Retta favored sedate dogs as well as sedate children.

Faye left long before we did. Cramer would do the driving required to get the horse to its new home. Faye had quipped, "I'm the horse whisperer; Cramer's the horse chauffeur."

They planned to meet the retired vet in Mackinaw City and buy him breakfast in gratitude for his help. Retta, the girls, and I would meet them at the boat dock at nine, and we'd ride over together. While Faye and the men arranged for the horse's transport, Retta and I would show the girls the Island. By late afternoon we'd be back in Mackinaw City with the newest member of Faye's family.

The day was warm and sunny. When Retta picked me up in her Acadia, she and the girls had hats, and I realized I should have brought one too. Pansy had a Detroit Tigers ball cap that had probably once belonged to Retta's son Tony tucked into her jeans pocket. Iris and Daisy wore straw hats about as practical for the Island as diamond tiaras. "It'll be windy on the boat," I warned. "Caps would stay on better."

"These match their outfits," Retta said as if that settled the question completely.

Retta's phone interrupted my thoughts. She reached for it, but I beat her to it. "You're driving."

"It might be important."

I read the screen. "Tiffany is calling. How important can it be?"

"I should talk to her." Her hand flailed at me, but I pulled the phone out of her reach. "At least see what she wants."

I hit the icon. "Retta Stilson's phone."

"Um...Is Retta there?"

"She's driving."

A long pause told me the caller didn't see why that was a problem. "I'd like to talk to her."

"We'll be stopping soon," I said. "She'll call you then."

When I hung up Retta said, "I can talk on the phone while I'm driving, Barbara. I do it all the time."

"Why don't you use that hands-free thing?"

"It doesn't sound right, and everyone in the car would hear."

"Better than everyone dying because you're distracted."

She made a sound that indicated I was being silly. "I'll give Tif a call before we get on the boat. Look, girls! There's the bridge!"

Mackinac Island is a little jewel set in the waters of Lake Huron on the eastern side of the Mackinac Bridge. With no cars or motorized vehicles, the place feels like a step back in time. Most visitors reach the island by ferries that run frequently during the tourist season from either Mackinaw City, at the tip of the Lower Peninsula, or St. Ignace, at the northern end of the bridge.

Retta chose the transport line with the rooster-tail ferries, thinking the girls would get a charge out of it, which they did. As we surged through the choppy water she acted as tour guide, pointing toward St. Ignace. "That's the Upper Peninsula," she told them. "People up there are called Yoopers, and it got added to the dictionary as an official word this year." With a glance at me she added, "Spelled Y-O-O-P-E-R."

We'd had the discussion before, but Retta never drops anything. My preferred spelling is Y-U-P-P-E-R, which better suggests *upper*, but that isn't what the dictionary writers chose. Retta thinks it's funny that my spelling is wrong according to Merriam-Webster.

Shooting her a look, I said, "Let's go below before the wind blows someone overboard."

In the cabin was a large banner welcoming WALL to Mackinac Island. The letters stood for something I'd heard of but couldn't bring to mind at the moment. There's always some sort of convention on the island between May and October, and the weather was certainly cooperating for this one. Aside from some wind, which is normal for the straits, the day was perfect.

We docked less than an hour after we boarded, following herds of chattering people, most of them women, onto the road that rings the island. The Straits of Mackinac has a long history of commerce in furs, fish, and forestry products. Today's trade is focused on tourism, so fudge and souvenir shops abound.

There the streets were full, but we wormed our way along, giving the girls a chance to spend the mad money Retta provided. As we trailed behind them, uninterested in plastic replicas of the Mackinac Bridge and T-shirts with clever sayings, Retta observed, "The people seem better dressed than usual today. See those women in heels and skirts? And those ladies over there don't look like tourists. No tank tops or cargo shorts."

I muttered something neutral, uninterested in whether visitors to the island were fashion conscious or fashion clueless.

Within a half hour or so, each girl had chosen her souvenir. Daisy bought a fairy-thing with no apparent purpose, Iris (after much deliberation) got a book about Indian legends, and Pansy chose a sweatshirt that said Michigan: 100% pure. Relieved to be done with tchotchkes, I said, "Let's show these girls some history."

We started with Fort Mackinac, a relic of the days when Michigan was controlled by first the French and later the English. Daisy clung to Retta's hand when they fired off the cannon, but she loved the costumed re-enactors who demonstrated various tasks and crafts of bygone days. Pansy asked a hundred questions about voyageurs and Potawatomis and pemmican. Iris read every word of every sign. Though her diligent study slowed us down a little, I considered it well worth the time.

At noon we sat down on the hillside leading up to the fort, where the harbor lay before us like a picture postcard. From a tote bag she'd brought along Retta served up a meal fit for several queens: chicken salad and peanut butter sandwiches, zipper bags filled with vegetables cut in clever shapes, cheese in dice-sized blocks, and a half-dozen collapsible bottles filled with either lemonade or raspberry-flavored water. I wondered what it had cost her to schlepp that much weight around all morning, but she didn't seem to mind when the girls oohed and aahed at their choices.

Faye joined us late, but one look at her face told us things had gone well. "She's ours!" She was panting a little as she dropped down on the grass. "Doc Hopkins thinks she'll be okay. Her lungs are weak, so she can't pull anymore, but he says that doesn't mean she's going to curl up and die anytime soon."

"That's good." Retta handed Faye a sandwich, which she held in one hand, too excited to take a bite until she told it all. "Cramer and Dolly got to be friends right away. Since there's hardly room on Doc's boat for the horse and the two of them, Doc suggested we meet them in Mackinaw City around three o'clock."

Retta frowned. "That's only two hours from now. We'll have to hurry if we're going to walk up and see the Grand Hotel." Originally, Retta had had hopes of tea on the porch of the Grand, but that happens late in the afternoon, and Faye didn't want to hold Doc Hopkins up. The compromise was to let the girls see the longest porch in the world up close before we left for home.

Faye looked toward the harbor. "There! They're heading for the boat now."

"Can we go down there?" Pansy asked. "I want to see her."

Retta sighed at the delay but said, "You girls go along. Barb and I will clean up our picnic and meet you outside the Pink Pony."

Much as I don't like Retta assuming I'll do as she says, I didn't have a problem with waiting a day or two to be introduced to the horse. Faye and the girls headed down to the harbor, ducking through the crowds of pedestrians, carriages, and bicycle riders to get across and reach the spot where Cramer and a wiry older man led a gray horse between them. The horse looked exhausted. Its head hung low and its steps were tentative. I had a moment of pity for the poor thing: old, sick, and being led out of its comfort zone. Still, it would soon be in a place it could only have dreamed of, if horses have dreams: no work, good food, and affection.

Doc Hopkins' boat was pulled directly onto the shore. It looked like a miniature version of the LST's I've seen in WWII movies, half raft, half boat. With deft movements the vet unhooked a chain at each side and a panel at the front dropped, forming a ramp for the beast to walk on. When he made a come-along gesture, Cramer led the horse forward. Hopkins took hold of her halter on the opposite side, and together they coaxed her onto the boat. Once she was aboard, Hopkins fastened the lead rope to the boat's stern. From the easy way he reassured her, I guessed this wasn't the first time Doc Hopkins had rescued an island horse.

"Looks like they've got things under control," Retta said behind me. "Let's get this cleaned up and get down there. It's a bit of a hike to the Grand."

Much of it uphill, if I remembered correctly. "We don't have to go up there. They saw the hotel from the ferry."

"You can't come to the Island and not visit the Grand." Her tone indicated despair at my inability to comprehend the good things in life. "These girls might get adopted by people who live in another state or who never leave home. We should show them what we can while we've got them."

I didn't like the thought of the girls moving away. I'd become accustomed to having them around, and I liked the feeling of being—not like a grandmother to them, but perhaps like an aunt.

With a sigh of acquiescence, I turned to helping Retta pack up our things. Retta does some things well, and today she'd served a simple but delicious meal with hardly any trash to dispose of and only a few items to carry home. If I were jealous of people who are clever at planning social events, I'd be jealous of Retta.

Brushing the grass from our rears, we stood side by side, looking toward the public harbor to see how the Dolly situation was progressing. I squinted, since the sun turned the water into a million tiny mirrors. Taking my sunglasses from my forehead, I put them on. It helped my vision, but I realized again that I should have brought a hat. My face was going to burn and I'd have the raccoon-eye effect for the next few days.

Digging in her purse, Retta came up with a tube of sunscreen and handed it to me. I took it, muttering thanks, and she smiled, pulling the brim of her pretty little sun-hat lower. She was feeling smart for having worn it, but for once she didn't say so out loud.

The horse was apparently secured and ready for her trip across the straits. The vet moved to the boat's cabin and nodded at Cramer, who loosed the moorings and hopped lightly over the panel, now upright again and presumably watertight. Dolly shifted nervously at the feeling of movement, but Cramer stepped up beside her and took her head onto his shoulder, petting her neck. Her back end shifted until she found her balance then she stared ahead stoically, obedient to the requirements of mankind.

"There," Retta said. "What time is it?" She took out her phone to look and squealed. "I got a text from Lars! How did I miss that?" Punching a key, she began reading, her face flushed with pleasure.

On the dock, Faye and the girls stood watching as the boat turned and headed out of the harbor. Daisy waved an energetic goodbye, turning her head slightly to say something to Iris. As she did, the breeze caught her straw hat and sent it spinning away. Before them a pier jutted out into the harbor in the shape of a T, creating dozens of docking slips for small boats. The hat rolled along its wooden surface like a wheel, heading straight for open water.

Faye called out something, and I thought I heard Daisy's cry of alarm. They froze for a second. Then Pansy sprinted onto the pier, chasing the hat. Twice it lost wind power and fell flat, but each time as Pansy approached, the wind picked it up again.

Thirty feet out, where the pier turned east and west, there was a small hut, perhaps for fish-cleaning. The hat disappeared inside it, and Pansy followed.

On the far side of the hut, two boats sat side by side. One was a fishing boat with the necessary tackle visible on hooks along its sides. The other was much smaller, with an outboard motor and no visible equipment. I couldn't see the front of either boat because of the hut. As I waited for Pansy to emerge with the hat, I heard an engine start. One of the boats backed away, turning as it went. I saw the pilot, a man larger than most who seemed likely to swamp the thing. His hulking shape was familiar, and my heart lurched in my chest.

"Barbara Ann, that's your phone." Retta's thumbs sped across her keyboard, answering Lars' text. I didn't move, staring at the spot where Pansy had disappeared, hoping desperately to see her emerge from the hut. "Barbara," she repeated. "Your phone!"

As I took out my phone, I tapped Retta's shoulder to focus her attention on what was going on below us before I answered, "Barbara Evans."

"I've got the girl," a voice said. "Let's you and me make a deal."

"What?" My mind raced, trying to absorb what was happening.

"If you stay where you are and keep quiet, we'll let her go in Mackinaw City. Any sign of trouble, we throw her into the straits and you can fish her out."

As I tried to put together what I was hearing and what I was seeing, the call ended. The smaller boat was almost out of the harbor, and the larger boat was now backing away from the pier. Leaning out the cabin window was a man with dark, curly hair. He waved as if in friendly farewell, but in his hand was the Tigers baseball cap Pansy had been wearing.

CHAPTER FIFTY-SEVEN

Faye

Barb and Retta hurried down the hill toward us. I was shaking, Daisy was sobbing, and Iris looked as if she might faint. "Farrell called," Barb told us. "He said we have to keep quiet or he'll throw Pansy overboard."

Iris looked at me in horror for a second then turned to Daisy. "You have to stop crying."

That didn't seem possible. Daisy was sobbing, but Retta took her aside, kneeling beside her so they were on eye level and speaking earnestly to the child.

"Is everything okay?" It was a young man with a baby on his back and a pregnant wife at his side.

"She lost her hat," Barb said, pointing toward the water where the hat bobbed peacefully.

"Oh, that's too bad," the wife said. "Maybe someone with a boat will go out and get it."

"Yes," Barb said. "We'll ask." The couple moved off, and I looked at the crowds of people. How had no one seen Pansy being kidnapped in broad daylight? The man on the boat had caught her off-guard. I recognized the name on the gunwale: *Mr. A.I.*

If it weren't for me, Pansy would be safe at Retta's house this very minute. I was near hysteria, but I told myself that wouldn't help anything. I had to be calm like Barb, who studied the harbor as if the key to all knowledge was out there.

Retta joined us, holding Daisy's hand. "She says that's Floyd Stone in the smaller boat."

"Pansy came face to face with them. They had to grab her or give up on the whole idea."

"What idea?"

"Today's the day they've been planning for all along." Barb lowered her voice so no one around us heard. "It was Farrell who called. Farrell and Stone are going through with the attack."

That started Daisy crying again, and Retta took her hand. They walked down the shore, Retta speaking softly to calm her down. Grateful as I was to Baby Sister for giving Barb and me time to think, all three of us needed to work on this together.

"Can you help with Daisy?" I asked Iris. Giving us a look that said she knew she was being left out of things, she went.

"They're operating on the fly now," Barb said when she was gone. "Whatever they have planned requires two boats, and it's going to happen soon."

I checked my watch. "Remember? Gabe heard Farrell say they'd meet on the dock at 1:00."

Barb glared after them. "They'll speed things up now. Farrell will know we'll call for help eventually, no matter what he said."

"Because we know they won't really let Pansy go free."

"Right. We've messed up their plans again. They probably have a way to escape worked out, but Pansy isn't part of it." Barb licked her lips. "I wish we knew where they're headed."

I stared out at the water, trying to think. "What's WALL?"

She chewed on her lip. "I was invited to join them when I first moved back to Michigan. I'm not much for—" She stopped, her eyes wide. "It's something about women in leadership, Women As—something that starts with L— Leaders."

"Floyd Stone told the postmistress about a conference for prominent women and female community leaders. She was surprised because he hated that she got promoted over him."

"And Gabe said Mindy was coming to a conference at the Grand Hotel." Retta had come up behind us. "Iris took Daisy to get cleaned up. I figured we needed time to make a plan."

Barb nodded. "Faye's going to tell Rory what's happening."

"There isn't time for that," Retta began, but a look from Barb stopped her.

"You will convince the local police we need a rescue boat as soon as possible. Men in two different boats are going to attack the women's conference at the Grand Hotel any minute now. Rory will back your story in case they doubt you."

"What about Pansy?"

"She has one chance of living through this," Barb said, "and that's if we stop Farrell before he blows up the Grand Hotel."

There were a dozen boats moored close by, and Barb pointed to a beat-up Starcraft with an engine that looked like someone had taken a hammer to it. "Is a boat like that easy to operate?"

Retta shrugged. "You start the engine, give it gas, and turn the tiller opposite the way you want to go."

"Okay." She frowned. "Don't just stand there! Go get the police!"

"What about the girls?"

"Faye will see to them."

I objected to being relegated to baby-sitter, but someone had to do it. Retta was the obvious choice to deal with policemen, men being the operative term. Barb had something in mind. I guessed I wouldn't approve, but I had to trust her. Time was ticking away.

Retta left to find the island police, moving quickly through the crowd. I followed Barb to where the owner of the Starcraft was loading fishing tackle into it. "How much for your boat?"

He glanced at us then turned away, clearly disbelieving.

"I'm serious," Barb said. "How much?"

"Four hundred dollars." It might have been worth half that. The guy's expression said he was going along with the joke.

"Will you take two hundred in cash and a check for the rest?"

He looked to me as if to ask if Barb was insane. "She means it," I said. Making a quick assessment of the man's character I added, "We're private detectives, and we need to follow some guys."

Only a short time later, Barb was climbing into the boat. The guy started the engine for her, gave a quick demonstration of how it operated, and stood back. Barb looked at me, fear and determination in her eyes.

"Maybe we should wait for—"

"We can't be sure they'll get there in time," she said. "Just make that call to Rory."

CHAPTER FIFTY-EIGHT

Retta

When I reached the island police station, a little out of breath, I told the succinct story I'd rehearsed in my mind along the way. "My name is Margaretta Stilson, and I work for the Smart Detective Agency. We've uncovered a plot to attack the Grand Hotel and disrupt the women's conference that's going on there."

The guy at the desk looked at me, clearly confused. I went on, "You must have gotten word recently of a possible plan to use a stolen grenade launcher."

He glanced at a bulletin board beside the desk. "Yeah, but—"

"We just saw two of the men involved in the plot down on the dock. They each have a boat. I don't know which one has the weapon, but they took a little girl hostage."

To his credit, the young officer tried to take it all in, but he wavered between belief and disbelief. The phone rang beside him, and he glanced from me to it. "Take the call," I said. "It might speed things up."

He answered, listened, and said, "Yes, Chief." Glancing at me he said, "Yes, she's here." More listening. "We have a boat that's always ready to go. ... All right. ... I will." He was halfway out of his chair as he hung up the phone. "Ma'am, you can wait right here."

"No, I can't," I told him in no uncertain terms. "My sister's out there trying to stop those men, and you're not leaving me behind."

CHAPTER FIFTY-NINE

Faye

Once I called Rory and told him the situation, Iris, Daisy, and I were at loose ends. Barb had steered the boat, clumsily at first but with growing confidence, out of the harbor and down the shore. Soon she was out of sight. My anxiety level rose.

Iris went to the end of the pier and watched until Barb was no longer visible. "If we walk along the road," she said, pointing west, "we can at least see her. Maybe we can do something to help."

It was probably a bad idea, but it satisfied my anxious heart and nervous feet. "We'll stay in the trees," I said. "If they start lobbing grenades, we'll take cover."

If I sounded like a John Wayne movie, it's because I've seen every one. Seven times, minimum.

We hurried through the crowded downtown, Iris pulling Daisy along. People turned to stare after us, and no doubt we appeared to be fleeing the zombie apocalypse. Gradually the crowds cleared. The road changed from Main Street to Lake Shore Drive. We could see the water again. The *Mr. A.I.* lay at anchor some distance out, pulling gently against the rope that held it in place. Closer to shore, in the smaller boat, Stone stood with his feet wide apart. He was bent over, working at something with focused intent. Barb and her ancient Starcraft were nowhere to be seen.

"What's he doing?" Iris whispered.

"I'm not sure."

I could see now that Stone wore a wetsuit. When I saw a hatchet in his hand, I realized he was knocking a hole in the bottom of his boat. I imagined the next few minutes. As the smaller craft filled with water, Stone would fire the grenades, one after the other. At the hotel, chaos would result, and it would be some time before anyone realized where the attack was coming from. While everyone was looking toward the explosions, Stone would drop the weapon into the sinking boat, abandon it, and swim to Farrell's boat, where he'd change into dry clothes. In a matter of minutes they'd be headed away from the disaster they created, appearing to be fishermen in search of a likely spot.

Movement on the larger boat caught my eye. As Farrell watched Stone scuttle his craft, Pansy had opened the window at the front of the cabin. Her head emerged first, then her shoulders, torso, and finally her legs.

"Look!" Daisy said. "It's Pansy!"

Iris shushed her, fearing she'd attract the attention of Farrell or Stone. "Ms. Evans will get her back, Daisy. We just have to be quiet a little while longer."

I hoped she was telling the truth.

Pansy crouched on the hull of the boat, unsure what to do next. If she jumped overboard, Farrell would simply haul her back in. If she stayed where she was, he'd eventually notice her and return her to the cabin.

A final blow from Stone brought a spurt of water. The boat wavered briefly and began to sink. Widening his stance even more, Stone bent and picked up the weapon I'd last seen in Ben McAdams' bunker. Taking it from its plastic sleeve, he set it to his shoulder, flipped up the sight, and raised the muzzle, aiming over our heads and a little to one side. I didn't have to turn and look to see his target: the entrance doors of the Grand Hotel.

On the fishing boat, Farrell began raising anchor. It whirred upward, but he watched Stone, fascinated as their moment of triumph neared. I watched too, but in horror. Stone would get his shots off, and up at the Grand Hotel, people would die. Even if they didn't get away, no one could prevent the damage they were about to inflict.

Except for Barbara.

Over the putt-putt of the fishing boat's idling motor, I heard a second engine and turned to where the prow of a boat appeared from a slight indentation in the shoreline. The noise began low but growled to full after a clunky little choke. Our recent purchase bore down on Stone's boat, with a grim-faced Barb at the back. Though she had some distance to cover, surprise was on her side.

Farrell shouted something to Stone, who turned, his mouth open. The gun's muzzle lowered. At the same moment Farrell saw Pansy kneeling on the hull a few feet away from him and made a lunge for her. She scrambled back, though she didn't have far to go.

"Jump, Pansy! Water side!" Barb called.

Without hesitation, Pansy launched herself over the side away from us. I lost sight of her as Barb closed in on Stone's boat, aiming directly at its center with deadly concentration. Farrell looked from her to Stone, frozen with indecision.

Stone made a final attempt to complete his mission. Setting the grenade launcher to his shoulder again, he took aim, but Barb's craft smashed into the already foundering boat just as he pulled the trigger. The impact shook him, and the barrel rose sharply. The grenade went straight up, paused for a second, and fell back to the water. It exploded when it hit the surface, and the Boom! it made reverberated, hurting my ears.

As the water roiled around it, Barb's boat drove into Stone's boat, turning it onto its side. Hands waving frantically, Stone fell backward, hitting the water with a splash that matched his size. The weapon flew from his hand, hit the water a few feet away, and sank.

On the fishing boat, Farrell made his decision. Rushing to the cabin, he turned the boat south and gunned the engine.

At that moment I didn't care about Farrell. Searching the water near the two boats, I caught sight of Pansy's head bobbing on the far side, but I couldn't see Barb. My lungs stopped pumping; at least that's how it felt. Where was she?

I ran to the shore, calling her name. Part of me was aware that Farrell was getting away, speeding toward Mackinaw City. Another part registered Stone, flailing helplessly in the water. It didn't matter. I searched the water, trying to see through patches of reflected light. Where was my sister?

When I spotted her, it was some distance back from where she'd last been. She'd aimed the boat at Stone then jumped, probably at the same time she told Pansy to do so. The little Starcraft had done its job, but now it floated upside down, its hull crumpled like scrap paper. Never in my life have I blown four hundred dollars with less regret.

CHAPTER SIXTY

Barb

The waters of the Straits of Mackinac are seldom warm, and certainly not in May. The shock to my aging body was terrible; the thought of being immersed for even a few minutes was worse. It was a great relief, therefore, to hear an engine running close by and turn to see a police patrol boat coming toward me. Retta peered over the side, and for once I was glad she's bossy. If it makes people do as you say in an emergency, bossy is good.

Some yards away, Stone was calling Farrell's name to no avail. The boat was already far away, moving at top speed. Stone's cries turned to curses. I hoped Rory had gotten the word out along the lakeshores. If he had, there was nowhere for Farrell to go. The Coast Guard would find him.

I was pulled from the water and wrapped in a blanket. Pansy was next, and when she was rescued and wrapped, she came and sat beside me. We shivered together, and I put an arm around her shoulders, pulling my blanket over both of us.

"Thanks for coming after me." Her teeth chattered as she spoke.

"Thanks for jumping the right way," I answered. "I really didn't want to squash you between the boats."

She managed a smile. "I didn't want to be squashed either."

The officers hauled Stone out of the water and flopped him onto the deck like a record-breaking trout. One of the men removed his handcuffs from his belt with a metallic click. "Stay where you are, sir," he ordered, "and place your hands behind your back."

CHAPTER SIXTY-ONE

Retta

Rory had told Faye he'd meet us at the docks in Mackinaw City. By that time I'd called to let him know everyone was okay, Faye had already gone to the Trading Post and bought dry clothes for Pansy and Barbara. My sister looked cute in light blue sweats and fake-Indian moccasins, a nice change from her usual black or navy. Her hair looked cute too. Having some natural curl, it fell softly around her face after the dunk in the lake. I wondered if I could talk her into giving up the severe blow-dry she always does.

They waited in the ferry company's parking lot: Rory, Cramer, Doc Hopkins, and the horse. Dolly was the only one that didn't seem worried.

Barbara Ann gave a brief version of what had happened. When she finished, the old vet turned to Cramer. "They always make life this interesting?"

Cramer grinned. "Most days they're just three regular ladies. Some days, not so much."

Rory put one arm around Barbara and the other around Pansy. "Let's try for regular tomorrow," he said, "and the day after too."

News came from the Coast Guard that Farrell had been picked up along US-23 north of Cheboygan. "Stone is already blaming Farrell for everything, and I bet Farrell will blame Stone," Rory said. "It makes things easier when the bad guys start pointing fingers at each other."

"Cramer's going to put the horse into the trailer so we can head home," Rory told the girls. "He can probably use some help."

After they walked away Rory said, "The verdict on Sharky is murder, not suicide. The sheriff will be looking at Stone and Farrell as primary suspects."

"I figured that," I said, counting on my fingers. "First, Sharky didn't sound to me like the kind of guy who'd commit suicide. Second, if he was going to kill himself, why'd he go out to our cabin to do it? It's more likely he was waiting for the time to do their dirty deed."

"But Farrell and Stone knew the police were aware of Sharky's involvement," Faye said. "They hoped we'd conclude the plot was over when his body turned up."

"The last thing was the fact the grenade-launcher thingy was never found. If Sharky had it, the sheriff's men should have found it." I met Rory's gaze. "How am I doing, Chief?"

"Pretty well," he replied with a grin. "Add to that the fact Sharky had no gunpowder residue on his hand, and we've got a pretty good case for murder."

A phone rang, and most of us made reaching gestures. It was Faye's phone, and she crushed out the cigarette she'd been trying to keep the girls from seeing as she answered. "Hi, Hon. We're just about done here, so—" Her expression changed. "I'll be home as soon as I can get there."

Hanging up, she tossed the phone in her purse without conscious intent. "That was Dale. Harriet's had a stroke, and they're taking her to surgery."

CHAPTER SIXTY-TWO

Dale and I waited outside the emergency room together, saying little. I flipped through a magazine I wasn't reading. Dale sat with his hands on his thighs, flexing his fingers every so often as if preparing himself to do something. There was nothing to do, at least not for us.

I thought of other times we'd waited together, dreading what was to come. The night when Bill, then eighteen, hadn't come home, and we heard on TV there'd been an accident with fatalities. The day our middle son, Jimmy, called from North Dakota to say his wife was in labor with our first grandchild and the doctors were concerned for the baby. When Dale's dad had the stroke that eventually killed him. My father's death. My mother's death. Each of those times, we'd sat like this, waiting for someone to tell us if our lives would go on as before or change forever.

The worst for me was the day Dale was hurt. I left the three boys, then eighteen, sixteen, and eleven, in school, allowing them a few more hours of normalcy while I waited to find out if the doctors could relieve the pressure on their father's brain and save his life. It was the only time since I was seventeen that Dale wasn't by my side during a tragedy.

That feeling of aloneness was the worst ever, but before Dale came out of surgery, Retta had showed up with our pastor in tow. She'd left my side only to pick up the boys from school, tell them what happened, and bring them to me. By the time Dale was settled in I.C.U., I had my sons and my sister for support. Barb had flown home the next day. We'd spent those critical first forty-eight hours together, speaking little and hoping much, until the surgeons said with cautious optimism that Dale would survive.

Now Dale and I waited again. Such times are terrible, dreading the worst, hoping for the best. But they're also when we most certainly feel the bonds between ourselves and those we love.

What did I want for Harriet? Peace. What would she get? That was up to God, but I knew Harriet didn't want to return to the room at the nursing home, split down the middle by an imaginary property line and decorated with signs that said things like, Don't forget to ask for help!

If she had a choice, Harriet would tell—no, she'd order—the doctors to leave her alone and let her die. I knew that, as did anyone who'd spent ten minutes with her in the last five years.

A tired-looking man came out of the door marked authorized personnel only, his hair mashed from the surgical cap he'd just pulled off his head. "Mr. and Mrs. Burner? I'm Doctor Simon."

We stood. "I'm Faye. This is Dale, Harriet's son."

He nodded at Dale but spoke to me. "Mrs. Burner came through the surgery well. She's surprisingly fit for her age, but it only takes one tiny problem area to cause this to happen."

"She's going to live?"

His grin was surprisingly boyish for a neurosurgeon. "We don't guarantee our work when the patient is over ninety, but she seems to be doing well."

We didn't have to face Death today. Harriet would go on, for a week, a month, a year or more. I wasn't sure how I felt about it.

After Dr. Simon left, Dale took my hand. "I'm glad I've got you."

Like a lot of men, Dale isn't much for expressing his feelings. I know he loves me. He's told me he's grateful I "stuck with" him, as if I could have walked away after he got hurt. He seldom says those things out loud, and that's okay with me. I know people who say "I love you" ten times a day, all the time treating each other like dirt.

For us, that's marriage. Whatever comes, we face it together. When it gets really bad, we hold hands.

CHAPTER SIXTY-THREE

Retta

When the doorbell rang, I looked out to see Carla and Bill standing on my front porch. I invited them in and offered coffee. As I made it we chatted about Harriet, who will live to be two hundred, in my opinion. Bill reported she was already ordering everyone around, as usual.

As we talked, I tried to guess the purpose of the visit. Probably they'd come to tell me the farm was too much for them to handle. Bill's never stayed at anything for long, and I was pretty sure Faye had taxed his abilities to the breaking point with this project. She wanted horses, but I never heard Bill mention liking them. Added to that, farming is hard work. I prepared myself to hear that Bill and Carla would be moving back to Chicago and I'd need to find new tenants for the farmhouse.

I was so certain of what Bill would say I had to ask him to repeat what he did say.

"We plan to take the girls," he repeated. "We've applied to become foster parents. If things work out, we'll make it permanent."

When I couldn't think of a single thing to say, Carla said, "It's unlikely Bill and I will ever have kids of our own, but we can make things better for these girls."

Recovering my senses I asked, "Have you talked to Faye about this?"

"Yes, and Dad too." Bill's tone reminded me not to count Dale out.

"How about your brother?"

"Cramer's all in favor." Bill chuckled. "He says it would be a shame if they had to go live in a city somewhere."

I sighed. "It's nice of you two to want to do this, but it's a huge financial undertaking. Can you support three children?"

"We're pretty sure we can. We sat down with Cramer and figured out a whole year's budget, and while we won't get rich, we'll get by. Cramer's got some ideas that will hopefully pay off in the future, like offering activities at the farm, maybe class outings, hayrides, or a petting zoo. He also says reindeer antlers are in demand. Did you know both the males and the females grow them?"

Selling antlers and giving hayrides? They'd be living on a shoestring, but I got the sense they didn't care. Maybe having a place to settle into was worth more than inventing the next ecological masterpiece.

"What do you want from me?"

They glanced at each other. "We thought we should ask the girls if they want to be with us before we go any farther with this."

Though I felt a little stab at the thought of my house being empty again, I had no doubt what the girls would say. "I have one request for you."

"Sure."

"They need a dog."

"They can each have one if they want," Carla replied. "We'll visit the humane society and let them choose."

Bill touched her arm fondly. "I think the motto at Prospero's Farm is going to be 'The more, the merrier!'"

I'd been thinking of a purebred, but I realized Bill and Carla couldn't afford to pay very much for a dog. The humane society would have to do. "All right, then." I rose from my chair. "Let's get them in here and see what they have to say."

CHAPTER SIXTY-FOUR

Faye

You're never too old to be surprised by your siblings. I came home this afternoon to find Retta and Barb giggling like teenagers. When I asked what was funny, they came up with some lame joke, but I'd have sworn they were planning something.

My morning had been spent at the farm, where the Isley girls were settled in nicely with Bill and Carla. Of course there wasn't a lot of settling to do, since they'd simply returned to the house they knew well.

Pansy is fast becoming a horse nut, and it pleases my heart to see how tenderly she treats old Dolly. She's begun riding Anni-Frid and Agnetha, and neither seems to mind. Pansy sits a horse nicely, and she admits it might be because she's ridden a few reindeer in the past.

Iris and Carla have serious conversations about the garden, what's doing well, what needs extra care, and what should be planted now that it's mid-June. It's cute to see them with their heads bent together over a row or a diagram, Iris so fair and Carla so dark.

Daisy has a dog. After extended deliberation, she chose a middle-aged black Labrador retriever with one eye. "He needs me," she told Bill. "Buddy and Styx are nice, but this dog wants to live on the farm with us."

There will never be a lot of money. Prospero's Farm isn't meant to make anyone rich. I'll do what I can to help, and Cramer will no doubt contribute more than his share. The girls won't go without necessities, and I believe they'll be better off not having everything they see. They'll be loved, which is worth more than all the money in the world.

As Barb, Retta, and I chatted about the girls' future, I thought about ours. Barb has apparently had a change of heart, because she speaks now of the three of us when she mentions the agency. She also asked if I thought the Sleuth Sisters was a better name for our business than the Smart Detective Agency. I had to admit that I prefer Retta's proposal, though it's a pain to change the name of a business once it's started.

I also observe that Retta is trying not to be pushy. I see her put her fingers against her lips sometimes, as if reminding herself to keep quiet.

"Faye and I were approached by the city," Barb said as we sipped iced tea. "They suspect one of the contractors working on the new parking ramp is padding his expenses. The company is based in Indiana, so it will require travel if we take the job. I propose that Retta could do the preliminary research down there. Is that okay with you, Retta?"

She started to say something then made the little lip-stopping gesture. Turning to me she asked, "I could go if that works for everybody. What do you think, Faye?"

I wanted to ask, *When did the pod people come and replace my sisters?* Instead I said, "With your contacts, Barb's smarts, and my mad computer skills, I think the Sleuth Sisters can handle any job."

Have you read Book #1,

The Sleuth Sisters, yet?

You'll learn how the sisters started their detective
agency, found a long-lost murder suspect, and almost
went from three sisters to two.

How about Book #2,

3 Sleuths, 2 Dogs, 1 Murder?

When Retta's "gentleman friend" is arrested for
murdering his wife, she's angry and embarrassed.
Though the sisters would like to clear his name, Win
hasn't been honest with them. To save his life, and ulti-
mately their own as well, they brave a winter wilder-
ness, far removed from any chance of rescue. Three
determined women, with help from a couple of dogs
and a pair of horses, can do anything. Sister Power!

**Both books available from Amazon (print, e-book, &
audiobook) and Ingram (print only**